Vortex

by

Joy Brighton

This is a work of fiction. Names, characters, places, and incidents are either the product of the author's imagination or are used fictitiously, and any resemblance to actual persons living or dead, business establishments, events, or locales, is entirely coincidental.

Vortex

Cover Art by *Jennifer Greeff*

The Wild Rose Press, Inc.
PO Box 708
Adams Basin, NY 14410-0708
Visit us at www.thewildrosepress.com

Publishing History
First Edition, 2022
Trade Paperback ISBN 978-1-5092-3734-0
Digital ISBN 978-1-5092-3735-7

Published in the United States of America

"What happened? Where's Forrest?"

"We don't know. She was washed downriver in the flood," Dickson whispered.

My knees wouldn't hold me, and I sat down hard in the cold, wet sand with a painful groan.

Smith brushed a nervous hand over his hair and managed to continue. "None of us could see the storm yet, but we listened to the forecast and came down to the creek to make sure nobody was hanging out too close.

"A kid playing in the water got caught in the current and dragged downstream to a high spot on a sandbar. He was stuck in the middle and crying when we arrived. Before either of us had a chance to pull out our equipment, Forrest waded into the creek."

"It was only a few feet deep. Only up to her knees. We shouted for her to get out. To let us do it. She hauled the kid into her arms, but before she could get back to shore, all hell broke loose."

Grady had her cop face on, but I noticed the tension in her hands. This was bad. Real bad.

I swallowed the sour taste in the back of my throat and concentrated on listening, even though my heart pounded in my ears.

"The water was moving faster now. A branch broke loose above them, and knocked them both over."

Dickson pointed toward the big rocks midstream, now almost covered in churning black water. "Forrest didn't panic—didn't let the kid go, either. She pushed him up on those rocks. But she couldn't hold on."

"And the little guy?" Grady asked quietly.

"Tucked into his hotel room, safe and sound. We used the ropes to get him.

Praise for Joy Brighton

Joy Brighton has won multiple contests for her many works, including a first place in a Linda Howard and several placements in the prestigious Daphne Du Maurier for mystery and suspense.

Dedication

For Trouble and all the eagles.

PROLOGUE

Painful silence pulsed through my brain and haunted my dreams.

In the murky light of dawn, a half-grown boy peeks out of his bedroom door. He shivers in the cold. A bad dream about snakes woke him, and he's afraid. Afraid of being alone.

Barefoot, he clutches the front of his oversize T-shirt and hikes up a too-short pair of ragged sweatpants. His feet arch against the chill of the worn linoleum floor. No socks.

He brushes a hank of his straight, dark hair back off his face and rubs the sleep from his eyes. With one hand touching the wall to guide him, he wanders down the narrow hall into the apartment's small kitchen. The naked bulb over the sink lights the shadows of the room a greenish-blue.

"Mom?" He glances around the space. She isn't sitting at the kitchen table drinking her hot tea. Or in the tiny living room, looking out the window into the rainy morning.

He frowns, and his heart thumps more quickly. Shoulders hitched, arms clinging to his sides, he hesitates. The silence feels scary, and he shudders.

Hurrying back the way he came, the boy scratches on her bedroom door with his fingernail and calls for her again. His voice cracks.

1

More silence. A cold, dizzy fear roars into his head, and he breathes in shallow gulps. Mom would never leave him alone. Why doesn't she answer?

Using both hands, he turns the knob and opens her door. The streetlight from across the road filters a dull glow through the bent venetian blinds and throws crooked lines across her bed.

She's there. Sleeping.

Relief rushes through him like cool water over a dam. He smiles and runs across the room. He'll crawl under her covers and warm up.

A nasty smell twitches his nose, and he turns his head to one side to avoid it. His stomach feels gross, so he breathes through his mouth.

"Mom?" He stands next to her, waiting for her to toss back the blanket and let him climb in. Happily, he waits for her to stir.

She doesn't move.

He reaches out his hand and touches her cold, stiff shoulder.

"No!" I shouted into the dim light of dawn. My pulse pounded in my ears, and I gulped air in ragged chunks.

Hands clutching my twisted blanket, I pushed back against my pillow, then wiped the sticky sweat off my forehead. My nightmare.

"You're safe, you're safe," I repeated to the darkness. Safe in my room at the Trading Post. I could even hear my cousin George snoring next door.

I wrapped the blanket around me and tried to forget the dream, but I still felt the cold touch of my mother's skin. Could still see the sheen of death masking her wide-open eyes. Still hear my screams of terror. My mother was dead, and I would always be alone.

CHAPTER 1

"Not bad, Josh, for your first time driving down the mountain." My girlfriend, Forrest, released her seatbelt. She pulled the elastic tie off her long hair and finger-combed her bangs out of her eyes.

I yanked the brake on her old jeep, leaned back in the driver's seat and gave her my best insulted glare. "Not bad? That was perfect. I didn't even squeal ol' Tilley's tires on the hairpin turns."

Forrest shrugged, but then flashed me one of her amazing smiles. "You were great."

"I never thought that stupid six-month can't-drive-with-friends torture would ever be over." I tossed her the keys. "Now I can help drive, and we can take Tilley to school every day. Faster than the bus."

"Gran's still complaining about gas prices. She says the bus is more ecological." Forrest finger-quoted the last word.

I hopped out of the driver's seat and walked around to her side to open her door. Forrest liked when I did the gentlemanly thing. "I'll chip in. I earned a ton this summer at the Trading Post."

"You might have to. I'm out. I haven't worked at the hotel in months. Not since I started my internship."

"But it's over today, right?"

Forrest walked over to join me on the gravel, but avoided my eyes. "Sheriff Grady wants me to volunteer after school two days a week."

4

"What about cross-country?"

"She thinks I can do both."

Disgusted, I crossed my arms. "Oh, and you listen to everything good old Grady says?"

Forrest studied me carefully for a moment, and then spread her hand wide. "Josh, I need a scholarship if I'm going to be accepted at the U in two years. Grady will help me qualify for one if I go into Law Enforcement."

"Grady this, Grady…" I mimicked her tone.

"You're jealous?" Forrest said, eyeballing me up and down with surprise. "Of Sheriff Grady? She'd give you an internship, too. I asked her last week."

"Not interested."

Forrest clicked her tongue and huffed out a quick breath. "Well, I am. I love everything about being a cop."

She glanced down at the humungo black watch that almost fell off her arm. The one she started wearing not long after she started the stupid summer internship at the Verde Valley Sheriff's Department. The watch that looked suspiciously like the enormous, do-everything-but-wipe-your-butt watches all the cops wore.

Shaking her head, Forrest lifted her pack out of the back seat. "I need to get going, or I'll be late for Saturday morning roll call. It's the last one I'll make before school starts next week."

I shoved my hands in my pockets. Maybe I was freaking because she spent so much time at the cop shop. Maybe I was jealous.

"Josh?"

I didn't answer.

She stopped and studied my face. "You look shot.

5

More dreams?"

I stared at my feet, unwilling to discuss the nightmares that plagued me.

"Wish I hadn't promised to cease and desist with the mind reading thing. I'd seriously like to know what's going on in your head right now. You've been in a pissy mood for days."

"Ah, but you did promise." I faked a smile.

She stepped closer and snuggled against me. "And I keep my promises." She patted my chest.

God, she smelled good. I rested my hands on her slim hips and drew in another long breath.

"I know, no peeking. Besides, you'd know the minute I raised my hand to touch your thoughts. You always do."

Before I had a chance to reply, she reached up and kissed me gently.

I stroked her soft hair while she pressed against me. So warm, so soft.

She broke the kiss, but kept her arms around my neck. "Wanna keep Tilley for the day? You could pick me up after my shift."

I recognized the compromise and tried for a real smile. "Sure, thanks. You're working in the office today?"

"No. Dickson and Smith are taking me on patrol." Her waterfall eyes lit with excitement.

"So Grady finally gave you a reward for slaving all summer in the file room?"

"Something like that." Forrest turned to go.

"Be careful," I called.

She ruffled her hair and shot me a grin. "Silly. Nothing ever happens in Verde."

6

****

Since I was on my own, I used the morning to hike up the Verde River. I considered the red rock canyon my private space. Of course, it wasn't. The land was part of the Forest Reserve owned by the federal government, but few people ventured this far into the wilds of the desert. Besides, the weather was way too hot for tourists to be roaming through the arroyos with their expensive guides.

Three miles in from the trailhead, I stopped for a breather.

The desert looked thirsty. The tiny green leaves of the palo verde tree drooped in the heat. The saguaros had gotten skinny, the water stored in their trunks and arms depleted. Even the white flowers of the agave plant hung limply from their tall stems. The monsoon season was late.

Humidity hung in the air, a rare feeling in a place that usually power-sucked the moisture off your skin the minute you started to sweat.

I sat in the shade and downed half a bottle of water. I hadn't ventured this far up the red-walled canyon in a while. Not since Forrest and I found the dead body of the grave robber last year. Even though we caught the murderer, Forrest still refused to hike here. She preferred the trails around Jerome, where she and her grandmother lived.

I wasn't spooked by the creek, and since I had the whole day, I might as well get in a training session for cross-country. The season would start a few days after school did, and I was determined to win some races this year.

After a couple more miles at a brisk trot, I was

soaked with sweat. I untied my running shoes and stuck my feet in the cool creek. Ecstasy. The river ran slowly over the huge red boulders, trickling past the sycamore trees lining its banks.

I dug in my daypack for another bottle of water and studied the petroglyphs decorating the aged black walls of the canyon. Ancient people, *my* ancient people, had etched the engravings on the walls.

Blessings. Pleas. Stories. I traced the small, cloud-shaped drawing that hung over a group of stick figures. One of the people wore a headdress. Was he the shaman from that time? The leader of his people?

Wonder what he felt like being a shaman? Had he worried about the responsibility as much as I did? Other figures who followed behind the people had heads and bodies, but no legs. A chill roamed over my shoulders, and I snatched my hand back from the rough rock. Ghosts. Spirits who followed the people through life.

I rubbed the warmth back into my arms. Did they help? Or make trouble?

I downed another gulp of water. My own ghost caused his share of trouble. Sometimes, a whole lot of trouble.

I took another long drink and dribbled the last of the bottle over my head to cool off. Pretty amazing. After all this time, I could finally be so chill about a ghost. He'd haunted me since I was a kid, and helped me more than once, but the Magician hadn't said "boo" most of this summer. I smiled to myself. I almost missed my creepy dead guy.

I leaned my shoulders against the warm sand and shaded my eyes from the overhead glare of the sun. What was my personal spook up to? Would he reappear sometime this year and continue his plan to educate me in the ways of the Ancients?

I rubbed my eyes, suddenly feeling sleepy. Even though I'd worked hard this week, slaving for cousin George to restock the Trading Post, I shouldn't be so wiped out.

Arizona's tourist season would begin soon, and we needed to be ready for the snowbirds and their constant demands for native jewelry, hokey T-shirts, and cowboy hats.

I stretched out my arms and leaned back my head. Maybe I'd close my eyes for a minute.

****

A raindrop splatted on my forehead and woke me. Another hit my nose and dribbled down my cheek. I jumped to my feet. More drops pelted the sycamore leaves, disturbing the peaceful canyon.

I glanced overhead. The sky had filled with threatening black clouds. Shit. Lightning struck upriver, and thunder rolled down the narrow valley. Rain drummed down on my head in drops big enough to sting. I gathered my day pack and shoes and ducked under the narrow rock ledge nearby.

My stomach twisted. What an idiot. I'd fallen asleep in a canyon. An absolute no-no in desert survival.

The wind picked up and blew the rain sideways, lashing at the trees. Yellow leaves scattered. The river, now brown and muddy, had already risen several inches, covering the rocks I'd been sitting by only moments ago. Not good.

A large branch tumbled downstream in the rising water. Lightning flashed again. This time the thunder followed quickly, and I cringed at the noise.

My breath quickened. More water filled the canyon, more debris churned in the muddy flow. Flash flood.

I shivered, and not just from the cold rain. The monsoon storm would fill the canyon with raging water in minutes. I glanced behind me at the rock wall.

Damn. I'd have to climb.

I put on my shoes, but didn't bother with the laces. No time. The river rushed over my toes and snatched my backpack in the surge. I let it go.

I turned and jumped up the first step of the cliff, grabbing a handhold. The wind whipped my hair back, and I was soaked and cold in an instant.

The sky darkened, and it was only the lightning strikes that helped me find the next handholds. I climbed, nearly blinded by the rain. My arms ached, my feet slipped, and I gouged my chin on a sharp outcropping. Finally I reached a narrow ledge twenty feet up, and could stop to gather my strength and my breath.

My heart raced. The roaring water had chased me up the side of the canyon and still pulled at my ankles in its muddy rush.

Higher. I had to go higher. I stretched out as far as I could, but even then I couldn't reach the next handhold from the precarious edge where I stood. I wanted to scream for help, but who would hear me? Save me?

Gushing water flowed down the cliff from above, loosening the rocks under my feet. I'd end up back in the river if I didn't jump for it now.

I dug my toes into the ledge, gritted my teeth and

leaped. Scrambling up, I barely caught a hanging pine branch. The branch twisted under my weight, bent, and threatened to break. Pebbles and mud showered down on my face. Hands, arms, shoulders screaming with exertion, I dragged my body up to the higher rock shelf.

With the next lightning strike, I saw a small cave hidden behind the branches of a mesquite bush. On hands and knees, I crawled inside. I wiped the rain off my face and sank to my haunches, breathing like a dragon with no fire.

Right in front of the cave entrance, lightning struck again, blinding me, deafening me. The stench of wild electricity heated my face and burned my nostrils. It split the piñon pine in two, and the branch that had saved me disappeared into the muddy water below.

I crawled to the ledge and peered over. Would I have to climb again?

I didn't know if I could. My body ached. I shook uncontrollably. My hands were bloody, ripped by sharp rocks. I took a moment to regain my breath, and clamped my jaw shut to control the shivering. I would climb if I had to, all the way to the next world, if that's what it took.

The storm passed as quickly as it arrived. It rolled down the valley, and the thunder finally quieted to no more than a distant mumble. The rain still fell, but not with the same fury. Swollen with mud and debris, the river had at least stopped its relentless rise.

I was cold. I was beat to shit. But I was safe. I would wait out the flood.

George.

Oh, shit. I'd better call George.

I dug in my pocket and let out a groan. I'd stashed

my phone in my pack.

CHAPTER 2

The sun reappeared on the horizon almost as quickly as it had been blocked by the thunderstorm, but it would set in another hour, and I was still trapped on this stupid ledge. I watched the churning water below me. Yeah, it had dropped at least three feet in the past hour, but it would be impossible to get out that way before late tonight.

My stomach grumbled. Had to be more than a couple of hours since I'd eaten.

And because the river drowned my phone, no one knew where I was. I frowned into the bright sunset. George would worry as soon as it was dark. And what about Forrest? A shiver rippled over my shoulders. I'd promised to pick her up after her shift. Had to be way past five by now.

Although my shoes were still soggy, my clothes had almost dried in the warm breeze. I slurped a mouthful of fresh rainwater from the depression in the rock near me. It tasted clean, but there wasn't enough to last for long.

In the intense shadows of the red-orange sunset, I studied the steep cliff behind me. A narrow ledge ran up toward the top. I shaded my eyes with one hand and squinted. With this brilliant last light, I'd be able to find handholds along that path. Then I'd pull myself up the rest of the way to the mesa using the wind-twisted pines

13

near the top.

I rubbed my hands on the back of my jeans. Time to climb.

I cinched my laces, but kicked out a loose rock when I scrambled to my feet. It tumbled over the ledge and made a huge splash before disappearing into the rushing creek below.

Only then did I notice the large hole under the boulder. Some animal would have to find a new den, now his cover was blown.

The diamondback raised his scaly head and searched the area with his tongue. I sucked in a breath while my terrified legs wanted to run.

No. Stay still. Don't move.

The rattler uncoiled, and his tail shook an ominous warning. He was a big guy. Ten feet at least. I gulped down my fear and remained motionless. *Move on, old friend.*

After an endless moment of staring at me with his unblinking eyes, the snake slid down a rock and slithered off in search of new digs. Only then did I breathe.

I peered into the dark hole, and my heart raced even faster. Not only a den, but a hiding place.

A leather-wrapped bundle was wedged into the bottom of the depression. I double-checked that the hole wasn't occupied by something even more unfriendly than brother snake, and then reached down to grab the package.

It didn't weigh much. I undid the leather thong, unwrapped a small water pot and let out a long, low whistle. But when I touched the pot, I shouted with pain, almost dropping it. The heat reddened my finger.

14

Even through the leather wrapping, the pot pulsed with power

Holy shit. It was *the* water pot. In the dimming light, I recognized its intricate black and white design immediately. And the ugly face carved into its surface. It was one of the sacred objects I returned to the Magician's grave when I was twelve. And it was as ancient as the old ghost himself.

****

Three cop cars were parked in front of the Trading Post, their lights flashing blue, then red, then white against the dark walls of the store. Sheriff Grady's SUV was parked across the street.

I let out a groan. Man, I was in for it now, even though none of this was my fault. Well, mostly not my fault.

With the precious pot tied in my sweatshirt, it'd taken at least an hour to climb the steep ridge to the top of the mesa, and then a couple more hours to walk the dark trail home to Verde. I ended up hoofing it all the way to the bridge over the highway and then back into town.

No way could I reach Forrest's jeep on the far side of the river. I only hoped her precious pink polka dot jeep hadn't been swept away in the storm. She'd never forgive me if I lost Tilley.

Cold and tired and starving, I crossed the quiet, rain-soaked street. It was way past closing time, but the lights were still on in the front of the store.

"I'm so busted," I said to the rising moon.

I dodged around to the alley at the back of the store. Thankfully, the door to our living quarters was unlocked. I took off my shoes and slipped inside. With

15

my pulse choking my throat, I closed the door without making a sound, dashed into my room, and hid the precious water pot under my winter clothes in the bottom drawer of my dresser.

I peeked between the curtains and heard Cousin George's deep voice. "You found Forrest's jeep at the trailhead. They must be somewhere near the river. You need to be searching…"

"We'll have a team there at first light." Sheriff Margaret Grady sounded calm but firm. She couldn't have been more than five feet tall, but the sheriff was definitely in charge of the room. Something about her face, the way she wore her blond hair in a tight bun, the way she moved with grace and power, had every other officer and even George listening and waiting for her orders.

"We can't…

"Mr. Kwail…George, I know you're worried, but I can't risk my deputies in the flood. I still have one of my teams unaccounted for."

George pulled on one of his silver braids and growled his disagreement.

"The water level will drop by morning. Josh is a resourceful kid. He knows the desert. He'll be fine."

I pinched my lips together and blew through my nostrils. Might as well face this confrontation.

When I stepped through the curtain, Grady was the first to catch the movement. "Josh?"

"Sorry, George." I stepped forward. "I came home as soon as I could."

"Josh," George shouted. He rushed over and grabbed me by the shoulders. "Are you okay? What happened?" Then his worn face changed from relief to

16

fury. "Where the hell have you been?"

Grady moved closer. "Are you okay, Josh?"

I nodded. "I got caught in the flash flood."

"You know better than to walk in a riverbed during a storm," George yelled in my face. "That's just plain stupid."

Ears burning, I stared at the floor. He was right this time. "I fell asleep. Never saw the storm, not until it was on me. I had to climb the cliff."

"Good thinking." Grady patted me on the back. "Better take care of those scratches now."

I touched my face and the sting reminded me how banged-up I was. My hands hurt worse.

George must have noticed me wince. "Did you fall?"

"No."

Grady looked around, her dark eyes searching behind me. "Did Forrest head home to her grandmother?"

"Forrest?" My stomach lurched, and I swallowed quickly. "Forrest went out today with Dickson and Smith. They promised to take her on a ride-along."

"Damn," Grady grabbed her com and rushed toward the front entrance.

****

I caught up with the sheriff before she closed the door of her big SUV. "Wait. Where's Forrest?"

"Don't know."

"But…"

"Dickson and Smith must have let Forrest ride along without my permission. They know better than to take a civvy on patrol, even an intern," she grumbled under her breath.

Then she turned back to me. "Radio's out. I called dispatch on my phone. They haven't been heard from in hours."

I needed to puke and took in a quick breath to push back the dry heaves wrenching my empty stomach.

"They haven't checked in?" George asked as he took me gently by the shoulder.

"It may be nothing." Grady held out her palm and tried to reassure me. She didn't pull it off. "The storm blew out the transmitter up on Mingus Mountain."

George's warm arm pulled me close, and I realized I was shivering. Forrest. I had to find her.

"Where'd they go?" I choked the words through my tight throat.

"Last time the team made contact, they were heading out to the river. Upstream near the freeway. Some tourist was wading in the creek, and his kid got swept away right at the beginning of the flash flood. Forrest…"

From the look on her face, there was more bad news, but I couldn't ask right now, with my throat closed up tight. No words were getting through. No air, either.

"We're coming with you." George grabbed the back door to the SUV.

Grady started to shake her head, but then relented.

"Come on." George almost threw me into the back seat.

I felt stunned, like I wasn't really there, wasn't really sitting in the cop car. "We have to find her, George," I finally managed to say.

"We will, son. We will."

****

18

Despite the terror pulsing through my system, I must have zoned out on the ride north. Even when Grady turned on the lights and siren and we hit ninety roaring onto the freeway, I sat there. Numb.

When we finally reached the last location called in by the cops, I booked it out the door of the SUV the minute the tires squealed to a stop.

I sprinted, almost tripping over the rough terrain, until I reached the flooding edge of the churning river. Emergency lights illuminated the shoreline, and few spectators hung out on a nearby picnic table. By now it was two in the morning.

"Where's Forrest?" I shouted to the cops over the roar to the still-flooding river.

Grady, flashlight in hand, moved more slowly, more deliberately. As soon as she stood in front of Dickson and Smith and crossed her arms, the officers hung their heads like a couple of whipped dogs. "Fill me in," she ordered.

Dickson, the younger of the cops, looked ready bust out and cry. "We told her to stay back."

"Can it, Dickson. It's our fault." Smith was bigger, older. Obviously the senior partner, he was a heavyset, clean-shaven, ex-army guy. He could probably take on the Taliban singlehanded, but his face was gray with worry.

"You bet it is," Grady said with an ominous tone.

"We wanted to…" Dickson again.

"You wanted to show off." Grady propped her hands on her duty belt and leaned in. "Big, tough deputies. Driving around in your big, tough cop car."

Even Smith's face had turned bright red by this point. Looked like Dickson might cut and run. Either that or puke.

"This doesn't matter now," I shouted in frustration. Ready to pound the idiot cops, I lunged at them, but George held me back. "What happened? Where's Forrest?"

"We don't know. She was washed downriver in the flood," Dickson whispered.

My knees wouldn't hold me, and I sat down hard in the cold, wet sand with a painful groan.

Smith brushed a nervous hand over his hair and managed to continue. "None of us could see the storm yet, but we listened to the forecast and came down to the creek to make sure nobody was hanging out too close.

"A kid playing in the water got caught in the current and dragged downstream to a high spot on a sandbar. He was stuck in the middle and crying when we arrived. Before either of us had a chance to pull out our equipment, Forrest waded into the creek."

"It was only a few feet deep. Only up to her knees. We shouted for her to get out. To let us do it. She hauled the kid into her arms, but before she could get back to shore, all hell broke loose."

Grady had her cop face on, but I noticed the tension in her hands. This was bad. Real bad.

I swallowed the sour taste in the back of my throat and concentrated on listening, even though my heart pounded in my ears.

"The water was moving faster now. A branch broke loose above them, and knocked them both over."

Dickson pointed toward the big rocks midstream, now almost covered in churning black water. "Forrest didn't panic—didn't let the kid go, either. She pushed him up on those rocks. But she couldn't hold on."

"And the little guy?" Grady asked quietly.

"Tucked into his hotel room, safe and sound. We used the ropes to get him off the rocks before the current got too bad, but we couldn't see Forrest. The canyon's too narrow, too flooded to hike down."

"What about a chopper?" I asked.

"I'll order one, but it'll be morning before they can fly."

Too long. I stared at the rushing water and bit my lip to keep from cussing. Forrest hated when I cussed aloud.

Grady knelt in front of me. "Don't worry, Josh," Her face and her voice softened, no longer the sheriff, but a friend who was as concerned—no, as scared shitless as I was. "You might as well go home. I can have…"

"I'm staying here."

"There's nothing…" George began.

Were they kidding? I wasn't moving until Forrest was safe. "No," I insisted. "I'm not going anywhere. I'll help search as soon as it's light."

CHAPTER 3

I was going crazy, but all I could do was sit on my butt until the water subsided. Sunrise came and went. The helicopter made several passes, with nothing to show for it.

Midmorning heated to noon, and I moved to a patch of shade. George had called Forrest's grandmother, and my Aunt Gina would sit with her until we found Forrest.

George offered me a bottle of water, but I shook my head.

He frowned and crossed his arms over his barrel chest. "You want to be useful when it's time to search for her? Then don't be a damn martyr. Drink this. I'm not going to carry you down that creek."

I stared at him but took the bottle and chugged the whole thing.

"Better. Now eat." George pointed to a table in the shade. "Some of the ladies in the tribe brought food for the search party. If you don't eat something, they'll be offended."

I shot him an I-don't-care-who-I-offend glare, but hauled myself over to the table. The sandwiches tasted like wood dust. I choked down three small bites, but my stomach threatened to revolt. I smiled briefly into the women's hopeful faces.

"We're all saying prayers," they whispered, and patted my hand.

I nodded, grabbed a couple of lukewarm colas, and chugged them for the caffeine. I needed to keep myself awake.

The press arrived. Two scrawny reporters craned their necks behind rows of yellow tape barriers. A heavyset guy pointed an ancient video camera the size of a minibus in my direction. I ignored their pleas for a comment and returned to my patch of shade.

Next thing I knew, a man in a pair of shiny cowboy boots stood next to me. Nice lizard, with silver-covered toes. Megabucks.

I shielded my eyes from the hot glare of the late afternoon sun and then stood to be polite.

Behind the barrier, the press went crazy as the well-dressed man approached me and patted my shoulder. "Name's Patterson." He shook my hand. "State Senator Lawrence Patterson. I came over from the county seat in Prescott when I heard. Anything I can do, son?"

I nodded but could barely listen, much less answer.

Finally he left me alone, walked over to George, and spoke with him a minute before he drove off in his big black Suburban.

I got up and paced like a panther I'd seen at the zoo. The debris-strewn river was still flooding, but now held within its banks.

Soon.

My heart heaved. Was Forrest cold?

Was she scared?

Was she struggling against the powerful flood?

The longer I waited, the more horrible my fears became.

****

Three eons later, afternoon turned to evening and finally, finally the water subsided.

"I can't wait. I'm going tonight." I threw a borrowed pack onto my back, cinched the straps, and buckled the belt. I had a radio, water, and a first aid kit. Hopefully, I'd only need the first two.

I grabbed a flashlight, extra batteries, and a stack of energy bars from the supplies in Grady's trunk. Forrest would be hungry when I found her.

"It'll be dark in less than an hour," George argued.

"Then let's get going," I shouted over the helicopter doing a final pass upstream before they lost the light.

Thankfully, the cops agreed, and we headed out.

I hurried along the dripping creek bed, running when I could, and dodging the slippery rocks and broken tree branches. In spots, I had to wade through waist-deep muddy water choked with debris.

I heard George grunting behind me. "Slow down. We don't want to have to haul you out, too."

Dickson and Smith searched the opposite side of the soggy bank. Sheriff Grady stayed at her truck to monitor the search. A canine team was hiking up the south branch of the creek. We'd work our way toward the middle of the ten-mile canyon.

"Forrest," I shouted into a narrow rock walls. Her name bounced back at me. I kept moving.

I was able to move faster over the debris than the rest of the team. After thirty minutes, I checked my GPS location and called it in to Grady.

"You're -ing too fa-, Jo-." Grady's voice crackled over the radio. The reception was crap this deep in the canyon.

I climbed up on a tall rock, hoping I could hear better. "Say again."

"Too fast." She repeated.

"So?" I had to find Forrest. Get to her. She could be hurt.

"Josh, slow down, you could miss something important."

"Roger." I tried to summon the patience George was always hammering at me about. I slowed my steps. Stopped to examine each crevice. Carefully, I worked my way downriver, searching under whatever debris I could lift.

I called her name until I was hoarse. The team behind me had moved down the fork of the canyon running parallel to the one I searched, and George went with them. We planned to join up again a mile downriver, near the Ruined City, an ancient Anasazi cliff dwelling.

Going this slowly had one big-ass problem. I wasn't getting to Forrest fast enough.

The radio was silent, too. No one else had had any better luck.

The last of the golden light disappeared from the upper cliff.

I searched.

The blue twilight drew down, limiting the visibility to no more than a few feet.

I shouted her name.

A narrow strip of moonlight lit my way for another hour, but then the stars and my flashlight were my only company. They weren't a hell of a lot of help.

"Forrest." I tried to call, but my voice was shot. I checked in one last time, worked my way up the ravine to an almost-dry patch of sand, and settled down for the night. My sugar buzz had fizzled, and my body ached with fatigue.

Digging in my pack for water, I discovered a space blanket—one of those lightweight, shiny things in a little package. I wrapped up the best I could and tried to rest.

****

"Josh?"

"Huh?" I stirred and tried to swallow against my parched tongue. Someone nudged my shoulder and called my name again, but the words were very far away.

The kiss did it. My eyes flew open, and I sat up straight.

Forrest giggled. "Good morning, Sleeping Beauty."

"Forrest?"

"Yep."

I grabbed her by the arms and gave a shout. I wasn't dreaming. "Are you okay?"

"Yep. Just a little hungry. Do you have anything in that pack a starving girl could mooch?"

"Sure." I still couldn't believe she was here. Safe. I rubbed my knuckles over my eyes and blinked a couple of times."

"Want me to pinch you?"

With a shout, I stood, picked her up by her waist, and swung her around.

She laughed with me and hugged me back.

Then I noticed the bandage on her left arm. "Jeez, you're hurt?"

"Only a scrape."

"But how?"

She picked up my backpack and took my hand. "Let me show you."

Finally, the adrenaline in my system began to subside, and the tingling faded from my fingers. Forrest was alive. Safe. I could draw in a full breath of air.

Then anger, hot and scared, flashed through me. I clenched my jaw. "What the hell were you thinking?"

Forrest glanced up at me and her waterfall eyes suddenly narrowed. "Is the little boy okay?"

"Yes."

"If I hadn't waded in when I did, he wouldn't be."

"But…"

"Josh." She turned to me, stepping close and putting her hands warm against my chest. "You, more than anyone, know that sometimes you have to take a risk to do the right thing. No, I didn't think I would get swept away, but I still would have waded into the river, even if I had known. I couldn't stand there and let the little guy drown."

That shut me up. I blew out a long, relieved sigh and stared at the ground for a moment. She was right. And so amazing. I put my arm around her and kissed her gently. "I'm so glad you're safe."

The radio in my pack crackled to life, although I couldn't understand more than every third word. " Can… noth…sign…"

I grabbed the handheld. "Shit, I forgot. I better let everyone know where we are."

"No, wait." Forrest put her hand over mine. "Let me show you something first."

"But your grandmother…everyone."

"Two minutes, Josh. Please." She led me along the sandy bank, working our way past a tight bend in the

27

river.

I glanced around. "How'd you get this far downstream and not get hurt?"

"I guess I got caught in the very beginning of the flood. The water was fast, but it wasn't filled with too much debris. I grabbed a branch to keep me afloat, and stayed in the middle of the stream."

I squeezed her hand tightly and gulped back the fear clogging my throat.

"But I was getting tired. I knew I wouldn't have the strength to keep going, so I tried to kick over to the side and grab onto a tree branch. I missed and went under."

Forrest stopped walking and finished the story. "Then an arm grabbed me and pulled me out of the flood."

"Who?"

She smiled a small, mysterious-follow-me smile. "You'll see."

I shrugged, and we continued downstream. Around the next bend in the river, I smelled smoke.

Then I smelled breakfast.

A skinny native kid, a couple of years younger than me, rose to his feet and put out his hand.

Forrest shot me a grin. "Josh, you remember Zalo."

"Good to see you again, Josh."

"Zalo?" I opened my eyes wide.

"Ya thought I was dead, right? Poisoned?"

"Well, yeah."

The boy laughed, showing a huge smile and friendly dark eyes. His hair was long and uncombed, and he wore nothing but a pair of beat-to-shit cutoffs.

He proudly thumped his skinny bare chest with both hands. "Doing fine. Forrest already told me about how you guys figured out who killed Morty, and then you caught Sheriff Robb with enough evidence to send him to jail."

"But where've you been all this time?"

Zalo spread his arms wide and grinned some more. "Right here."

I glanced up. We were standing at the base of the ancient cliff house.

"Since the sheriff wanted me dead, I decided to stay dead. At least until everything cooled down. Then, by the time I heard about his arrest, and it was safe to come back, I decided to stay on." Zalo gaze travelled up and down the canyon. "It's good here. Warm in winter. Cool in summer. There's plenty of water. Did you know about the spring?"

I shook my head. "But what do you eat?"

"Well, I could say I live off the land, and I do. Sometimes I sneak into town at night and…" he cleared his throat, "forage. Nobody locks their doors, so I take a little here and a little there. Your cousin George sure does bake the best biscuits. Every Sunday he makes a triple batch."

"Kinda cool?" Forrest nudged my arm. She sat down next to the fire and pulled a piece of cooked meat from the hand-built spit made of old coat hangers. "Want some?"

"It's squirrel," Zalo continued, biting off a big chunk and licking his fingers. "Lots of rabbits, too. Plenty of fish in the creek. Prickly pear's almost ripe. I was thinking about growing a little corn and squash next spring. Maybe some beans."

"Don't you want to come back with us? The sheriff's locked up. No one will hurt you now."

Zalo shook his head and continued to chew.

"I already tried that line, Josh," Forrest said.

"I was lonely at first. And scared, but now this is my home," Zalo said between enormous bites.

"You should see the great room he's fixed up in the cliff dwelling." Forrest pointed overhead. "It even has a nice straw bed and a totally awesome view of the river."

The radio crackled again, and I reached for it.

Forrest stood. "If Zalo doesn't want the world to know where he is, then we'd better head back."

"I don't like leaving…"

"Look, Josh," Zalo interrupted. "I'm fine. Really. I've lived here for almost a year and, believe me, it's better than anything I ever had before."

With a shrug, I relented, but I still felt nervous about leaving the kid behind. I turned to Forrest. "I'll call the other team. Let them know we're hiking out their way."

I radioed in, and Forrest grinned when the men up-canyon let out a joyful whoop. They would call back to base and let the rest of the search teams know Forrest was safe.

"Thanks." Zalo wiped his fingers on his cutoffs before shaking my hand "You'll keep my secret?"

"For now," Forrest said. "As long as you let us know how you're doing."

"Sure."

"Anything you need?"

"Maybe a batch of brownies sometime? I sure do miss my grandmother's home-baked brownies."

CHAPTER 4

I was so grounded. It was days and days before I was allowed to see Josh again. The whole weekend was a waste.

After Gran got over crying and being out-of-her-mind scared for me, she was really ticked. It didn't seem to matter to her that I'd saved a little kid's life, only that I'd taken a mega-risk to do it.

She even took away my phone. Now that's just cruel.

Finally it was Monday morning. I don't think I've ever been ready so early to go to school. When Tilley and I arrived in the parking lot, my heart did a happy little flip. Josh loitered by the steps to the library. He smiled, and I flashed him a thumbs-up before I parked Tilley and hurried over.

"How's your arm?" he asked, walking close enough to touch me once in a while.

I nudged him back. It was the best we could do for now. No PDAs allowed on campus. Not even holding hands. The new principal was a real bad-ass about the rules.

"Fine." I showed him the smaller bandage, and flexed my arm a few times to prove myself fit for duty. Then I stared into his melted caramel-colored eyes, and I couldn't help a miniscule, underground sigh.

He chuckled. "Me, too," he whispered in my ear. "Been a long weekend."

As soon as we entered the quad in the center of campus, a crowd gathered around us. My friends shouted a zillion questions at me, and pulled me away before I even had a chance to wave goodbye to Josh.

Josh and I have no classes together this year. Again. I thought it was a conspiracy, but he just laughed. He didn't believe in Area 51, either. So I'd have to wait hours to have a real conversation with him.

I loved talking to him. It was one of the best things about Josh. Sure, he was cute and tall, and turning into a real hunk. Plus he was smart and, of course, psychic. But I seriously appreciated when he listened to my dopey ideas like they weren't crazy at all. He got me.

The buzz about my rescue droned on all morning. By the time lunch rolled around, I was sick of the hero worship. We sat at the farthest table down and tried to act normal.

"Did you tell anyone about Zalo?" I asked as soon as we were alone.

"No way."

"I wonder if I should tell Grady when I talk to her again."

"And break a promise?"

"But what if he has family who are worried?"

Josh shook his head and stuffed another bite of ham sandwich in his mouth. He continued talking, looking like a lopsided chipmunk as he spoke. "When he worked for us, Zalo told George he was all alone."

I nodded, twirling one of my carrot sticks. I can never eat when I'm worried. "That's what he told Gran, too, but what if he was lying? What if he ran away and someone's looking for him? We need to do something."

"I wouldn't."

"Maybe I'll go check on him."

Josh let out a low groan.

"Come with me?"

The groan intensified, but he shrugged. "Okay, soon. But let's check the weather report first."

I laughed. Then I looked both ways and gave him a finger kiss, right on the lips.

****

Forrest left a text before I was up on Sunday morning.

Worried, but have a plan.

B in Verde by 2

I had my own worries. Late that morning, after George went out, I dug in my bottom drawer and pulled out the water pot.

I held it by the leather wrapping. For more than an hour, I stared at the intricate design of a strange-looking face with large eyes and a menacing frown. I wasn't ready to take on a reading yet. My barriers were strong now, and I wanted to keep them that way.

But something wasn't right. Every other time the Magician gave me a gift, he either delivered it in person, or he showed up within a day or two to give me instructions.

It had been more than a week since the flood, and he had yet to appear. No ghost had popped out of my bedroom, or even haunted my dreams. Was the creepy pot really from him?

It had to be. No way there were two of these ancient artifacts in the world.

Patience? At this point I had zip.

"Josh?" Forrest's soft voice called from the kitchen door. I hadn't heard her knock the first time.

"Hang on," I called. Stashing the pot, I tucked in my sweaters and shoved the drawer closed.

I went into the kitchen and grinned. "Hey."

She smiled back.

I bent down and kissed her lightly, but she grabbed me by the scruff and went in for a hot one. My heart raced and my ears began to buzz. The girl could kiss. I wrapped my arms around her waist and held her to me.

George cleared his throat, and we both looked over. He stood near the curtain separating our rooms from the store. "Guess I better learn to knock."

"Hi, George," Forrest said brightly and moved out of my arms to give my cousin a peck on the cheek.

His cheeks turned red even under his dark, sun-soaked tan. I snickered.

"I brought brownies." She picked up two plates covered with foil.

George dug inside and took a big, chocolaty square from the top of one stack. "Uh, thanks. I'll let you two have a few minutes." He dropped the curtain, and his footsteps moved to the front of the store.

I poured two glasses of milk and settled at the kitchen table to polish off the first plate. Forrest made brownies from scratch with nuts and chocolate chips inside. These were still warm. I was practically drooling. "Mmm," I sighed, chewing slowly through the rich flavor.

Forrest grinned. "You can eat one plate, but this batch is for Zalo."

"Are we going to take them all the way out to the canyon?"

"No." Forrest was obviously super-proud of herself. "Remember Zalo said he loved George's

34

biscuits?"

"Yeah."

"And what day does George always make biscuits?"

I flashed to the stack of Sunday biscuits still sitting on the counter and nodded.

"We'll leave Zalo a note. When he comes foraging, he'll get our message. We can meet after track practice tomorrow at the southern trailhead."

Before bed, I left an old sweatshirt, a couple of T's, socks, and shoes, a pair of too-short jeans, and some warm gloves next to the plate of brownies. It would be getting colder soon. A few hand-me-downs were the least I could do for the guy who saved Forrest.

****

Zalo was waiting for us Monday afternoon, sitting on a fallen sycamore log near the trailhead. I recognized the clothes he was wearing. He'd rolled the sleeves and turned up the bottom of the old pair of jeans, but with the help of a belt, he now had something warm to wear when the weather turned cold.

I gave Josh's arm a thank-you squeeze.

Josh blushed, but neither of us said anything to the boy. Pride is a fragile thing.

The three of us hiked upstream a mile for some privacy, and then sat in the shade of the canyon. Most of the golden sycamore leaves had fallen, and the creek bubbled quietly. It was cool in the shade, a welcome feeling, especially when you're new to surviving in a desert.

Josh had a worried expression when he dug down to find something in his backpack. He removed several layers of paper and bubble wrap, pulled back a leather wrapping, and uncovered a beautiful pot. Round and squat, it fit in his two hands, and had a dull but well-rubbed finish.

When Josh held it up in the light, a strange face stared at me from the pot's surface, and a ripple of surprise scampered up my spine. "Seriously?" I questioned him. "When did you find it?"

After a moment, Zalo gave a long, low whistle.

Josh narrowed his eyes and studied Zalo with an intensity I recognized. "You know what it is?"

"May I hold it?" I asked, and Josh handed me the artifact. The decoration was elaborate. I had seen something like this when Gran and I visited the Heard Museum in Phoenix. "How old?"

"Very," Zalo whispered, taking it carefully into his hands. He inspected every side.

"What do you know about it?" Josh asked.

"That's a long story."

Josh crossed his legs and rested his elbows on them. Apparently, we would be here a while.

Zalo turned the pot slowly one more time, but didn't look up at us. "Most tribes hand down legends through the centuries."

Josh hadn't moved. He'd hardly breathed.

"So is this a Hopi pot?" I asked. "Or Yavapai?"

Zalo shook his head. "It may have been owned by an Anasazi or an early Hopi at some point, but this was made much farther south. Maybe in what is now Mexico or Central America."

A chill crept over my shoulders. I scooted closer to Josh, and he took my hand.

"How old?" Josh repeated my question.

"Hard to tell. Could be Aztec," Zalo said under his

breath. "No. I have a feeling this is even earlier."

"How did it wind up here?" I whispered. We had all leaned closer together, hovering over the pot. A loud voice seemed—I don't know, disrespectful.

"Trade routes," Josh said, and Zalo nodded.

Zalo shifted and resettled, still acting nervous. Was he scared of the pot? I was tempted to take a read, but Josh wouldn't like it.

He finally glanced up. "Trade routes ran from Central America all the way to Canada long, before Columbus thought he discovered a new place."

Josh rubbed a hand over his face and pushed the hair out of his eyes. "So you think this was old when it was brought to the valley?"

Zalo looked straight at Josh and gave a silent nod. "Where'd you get it?"

Josh wrapped the pot with extra care. "Found it."

"Where?" I asked, even more curious, because he was acting so totally weird.

"Up on a cliff."

Zalo's mouth curved down, and he made a groaning sound. "Not good."

"Why?" I asked. I sat up a little straighter and curiosity curled through me.

Zalo pointed to the pack. "That, my friend, is one very powerful pot. Was it raining when you found it?"

"Pouring.

"The day of the flash flood?" I asked, squeezing Josh's arm tighter.

Josh nodded and took my hand in his. "I had to climb up the canyon cliff to get out of flood."

Zalo rubbed his nose thoughtfully. "And the rain got worse?"

"Nooo," Josh drew out the word. "Not really. The storm was moving on by then."

The boy glanced up and so did I, but the sky was a clear, deep blue. Not a cloud anywhere. I must have let out a sigh, because both guys chuckled nervously.

Zalo scratched his chin. "Well, I guess the pot doesn't start the rain, but I would bet it will bring more, if you know how to use its power."

"Is it a gift from the Magician?" I asked, before I remembered Zalo didn't know about Josh's ghost.

Josh gave me a quick are-you-kidding glare, but Zalo had already tuned in to my rash question. I covered my mouth with a hand.

"Has he returned? The Magician? I know many stories about him."

Josh let out a low groan. "I shouldn't tell you…"

Zalo gave an impatient grunt. "Then why'd you bring the pot?"

"I-I don't know." Josh finished wrapping the ugly thing and stowed it in the top of his pack. He frowned and stared at his feet for a moment.

I looked back and forth between the two boys, and suddenly got the strangest feeling. I raised my hand like I was shielding my eyes from the sun, and took a quick read on Zalo. Yes. Truth. My heart started beating so fast I couldn't catch my breath. "Josh. I think Zalo is supposed to help us."

Josh turned to face me, his brows drawn down over his gorgeous eyes. "Maybe. I'm not sure."

Zalo straightened his shoulders and looked even more interested. "Help you? Help you with what?"

"What could it hurt to listen?" I insisted.

"I know lots of stories," Zalo assured us, his eyes

lit with excitement. "I know all the stories from all the tribes."

"See?" I squeezed Josh's hand. "Zalo can help you learn more about the tribe's legends. I bet the Magician planned the whole thing. You know how…"

"…sneaky he is?" Josh finished my sentence.

On the surface, Josh didn't seem convinced. Then I looked a little closer. No, I didn't break my promise not to read his thoughts, but sometimes the truth hovers around a person and is almost impossible to miss.

Truth? Josh was hoping for Zalo's help. We both knew Morty, the guy Sherriff Rob murdered, had befriended Zalo. The thief had used the stories Zalo told him to raid ancient graves. Josh needed those stories too, but for the right reasons.

"Just think about it, okay?" I suggested as I got up and dusted off the backside of my jeans. "It'll be dark soon. We should get going."

"Let's meet Saturday," Josh suggested. He stood and swung his pack onto one shoulder. "Okay if we hike into the Ruined City? That way we can spend most of the day, instead of having only an hour to talk."

Zalo nodded. The boy turned to head upstream, but stopped and said over his shoulder, "Until then, be careful with the pot."

We walked back to the trailhead in silence. Josh climbed into the passenger seat, and I started Tilley. "Sorry I blew your secret about the Magician," I said.

Josh smiled and gave a shrug. "I would have told him anyway. If not today, soon. But you're right. Somehow Zalo's connected with what I have to do. I don't know how yet. I wish the Magician would show me."

I laughed as I downshifted and revved the engine to climb a steep rise. "First time I've ever heard you say you want to see your old spook." I dodged a huge boulder and a Grand-Canyon-sized pothole. We were making good time despite the washboards on the dirt road.

"I noticed you didn't mention our talents to Zalo," Josh shouted over the wind and Tilley's roaring engine.

"Zalo's very superstitious. He might need a little time to get used to the idea we're both psychic."

CHAPTER 5

Zalo had a rabbit roasting on the fire by the time we arrived at the Ruined City on Saturday morning. The smell made my mouth water, and I was starving after the hike downriver.

Forrest pulled three apples out of her pack to share. We sat near the fire, eating with our fingers. The rabbit was delicious, smoky and tender. I licked the grease off my fingers and sucked on a bone.

It had been colder last night. A front coming in from the west brought near-freezing temperatures. Zalo wore the sweatshirt I left for him last week, and a Bronco's cap he must have "foraged" from somewhere else.

"Have you seen the Magician lately?" he asked after he finished his apple, core and all.

"Not since he helped us capture Sheriff Robb at the burial site," I answered between bites of my own apple.

"Almost a year," Forrest added.

"Time is different for him," Zalo said.

I studied the boy's face. "Meaning?"

"Well, it's not like he gets up every morning and brushes his teeth and goes to work. He lives in a different place. A different world."

"So these months or years may not seem like a long time to him. Got it. But I still want to know what the hell is going on. Whenever he's left me a gift before, he's always appeared and somehow told me

41

about it, explained its purpose and taught me how to use the tool."

Zalo wiped his mouth with the back of his hand. "So maybe he'll let me tell you the story this time."

"You're not a ghost, are you?" I joked.

Forrest chuckled, reached over and touched the boy's arm. "No. Totally solid."

"And you just happened by to pull Forrest out of the flood?" I eyeballed his reaction, but he remained straight-faced and calm.

"And you just happen to know all about pre-Columbian pots?" Forrest continued. Her eyes narrowed.

"And I just happened to find the pot at the top of a cliff I had to climb after a rattler—"

"Snake? Rattlesnake?" Forrest squeaked.

"The rattlesnake's his totem." Zalo rose to his knees. "One of the Magician's animal forms is a snake. Have you ever seen one before when he was around?"

The chills ran up and down my spine, and it took a minute to find enough spit to swallow. "Couple of times in visions. My Uncle Kenny died because a big rattler jumped out and bit him. Seeing the snake caused him to fall off a cliff."

"You must have been in great danger," Zalo whispered.

"Kenny was trying to kill me."

Forrest sucked in a quick breath.

I warmed my hands by the fire for a minute and tried not to shiver. "Did the Magician have Uncle Kenny kill my mom?"

Forrest touched my hand.

"No," Zalo said. "Humans make their own choices.

42

Good and bad." He sounded pretty positive, but I wasn't sure I believed him yet, even though I wanted to.

Forrest studied Zalo quietly and then nodded. He was telling the truth. At least the truth as he understood it.

I let out a frustrated breath. "What a mess."

Zalo raised his hands over his shoulders and shrugged. "I don't understand much more than you do right now, but for some reason we've been brought together. Call it fate. Or luck…"

"Or the Magician's not-too-subtle conniving," I added.

"I think I'm supposed to help you." He settled back and chewed another mouthful of rabbit thoughtfully. "I'm a Story Keeper."

I glanced up in surprise.

"That's my job. My gift." He held his shoulders and chin proudly. "I can remember the old stories as soon as I hear them. Perfectly. I listen to the elders, and let them tell me what they know."

"Cool, Zalo."

"One time my grandmother took me to Mexico and Central America. I was only about seven. She never did tell me why, just said we were visiting family. We stayed with some people I called Aunt and Uncle, and they told me more stories. I think my grandmother knew I was to be a Keeper. She was one before me."

"What happened to your grandmother? Does she still live on the Hopi reservation?" Forrest asked gently.

Zalo dropped his chin. "She died about four years ago." Then he gave Forrest a sad smile, and she hugged him in return.

"It's going to get cold soon. Are you sure you don't

want to come live in town for the winter?" she asked him gently.

"George could find you some work," I continued her thought, "and a warm place to stay. Maybe you could go back to school."

Zalo shifted nervously and then stood. He shoved up the sleeves of his oversized sweatshirt. "You guys are the best. I haven't had many friends growing up. Guess I always acted pretty weird."

"We each have our own weirdness." Forrest shot me her you-know-what-I-mean smile, and I nodded.

Zalo sat back down. "Most people are a little afraid of me. They were afraid of my grandmother, too." Zalo stared at the ground. "They thought she was a witch, but she was just old and a little forgetful. Very superstitious. And well, maybe…a little crazy."

"Remember my grandmother?" Forrest chuckled. "Now *she's* a little crazy."

"Your grandmother's very kind," Zalo argued.

Forrest took him by the arm. "Come back with us."

He gazed around the canyon and up the walls of the old city. "Maybe later. I'll stay here for now."

* "Why haven't you touched the pot?" Forrest asked as we hiked back along the trail to her pink and red polka dot jeep.

"Can't sneak anything past you, can I?" I said with a snort.

We both climbed into her jeep. With her keys in her hand, Forrest sat staring at me intently. "You held the bowl with the leather cover."

I gave a noncommittal shrug.

She turned in her seat and examined me, head to hiking boots, with those expectant blue-green eyes. "I

44

thought maybe you didn't want to get the pot dirty, but then you let me handle it. Zalo, too."

I took the pot from the safe place in my pack and partially unwrapped it. She was right. I hadn't touched it since the food, and I didn't want to.

"I don't know," I continued to stare at the small, very ancient pot. "I'm kinda freaked. It burned my fingers the day I found it."

"Wow." Forrest took the pot from me and examined the decorations carefully. The ugly face on the pot stared back at her. "So if this thing is Aztec, or even older, it must have a ton of history."

I dodged the gust of fear blowing through me and let out a long sigh. I rubbed my palms together. "Guess I should find out."

She gave me a quick nod and held the pot in both hands. "Are you ready? If the vision gets too weird, just tell me, and I'll take the pot back."

I swallowed the mega-lump in my throat and prepared for the assault. I left my barriers mostly up, in case the vision was too powerful. I still didn't know the limit of my gift. Would I be able to see hundreds, maybe thousands of years in the past? Did I even want to?

Forrest settled the pot in my upraised hands, and at first I just felt the cool matte finish of the ceramic. I dropped my shields a fraction and sensed the heat, but because I was prepared, I could control the power this time. I let the pot show me the vision.

Fire.

But all pottery comes from fire. I looked closer. This blaze burned many years after the pot was made. I stood in a stone-walled room, dimly lit with flickering

45

torches.

Men in masks. Nightmare masks of strange animals.

My pulse thudded in my ears.

In the distance, a child was crying.

Fear. Blood.

I held a warm and moving thing in my hand....

"Take it back." I screamed. "Take it back."

Forrest snatched the pot from my hand, and the vision slowly faded.

Drenched in sweat and gasping for breath, I still smelled the copper tang of blood and fought to control my fear. I was gonna puke.

"Josh, I've got you." Forrest grabbed my hand and helped me push back the terror. "Come back."

I opened my eyes and examined her beautiful face. Her gaze held peace, and hope, and love. I sucked in a lungful of air, and my vision cleared. I laid my head on her shoulder, and she held me until I could speak.

"Wow," she whispered.

"I know." I rubbed my hands against each other and stared at them. They were clean, but still shaking.

"I saw the child," she said.

"You could watch?"

"I saw flashes of it." She swallowed and blinked back tears. "Was it a sacrifice?"

"Yes."

"You were holding a..."

"A heart..." I shuddered again. "A beating heart."

Forrest must have remembered she still had the pot in her lap. She gingerly laid it back in the leather wrapping before wiping her hands on her jeans. "Was there blood in...?"

"I think so."

"It's very old," she whispered. "Maybe older than the Magician?"

I blew out a breath and shrugged. "How old is the Magician?"

****

I needed a better place to hide the Magician's pot than the bottom drawer of my dresser. But where? Hands on my hips, I studied my tiny bedroom and frowned.

Should I take it to the salt mine? Frowning, I paced the ten steps across my room. Somehow the old salt mine didn't feel right. Too many people from the tribe knew I went there to pray. There had to be a safer place to hide the valuable pot.

I stared out my window at the muddy alley, feeling claustrophobic. It had rained for most of the past two days and nights, thunder cracking overhead. Water drops still blurred the glass of my small window.

I leaned against the wall. Everyone still thought the Magician's necklace was under beefed-up surveillance at the Jerome museum, just a nice piece of early Anasazi jewelry. Forrest and I knew mosaic of the saber-toothed tooth cat was the key to the Magician's grave, but only I knew where the real one was hidden.

The little courting flute was hidden at Rocky and Gina's place. I hadn't played it in months. Forrest was too susceptible to the draw of the music. When the time was right for us to be together, we didn't want some flute manipulating our real feelings.

I flopped on my bed and scrunched a pillow under my head. I didn't want to take the pot back to the burial site on the cliff side. My old ghost had given me these

47

artifacts for a reason, and I had to figure out what that reason was. Just like the flute and the necklace, the pot was connected to the power I would someday control.

I dug under my sweatshirts, unwrapped the ugly thing, and stared at it for a long time. I settled on my bed and crossed my legs. I needed to know more, and knew one place I could search for clues.

I chewed on my lip. Was it worth the risk, using my skill on my own? No one would pull me back if the vision overtook me. Curiosity outweighed fear.

Building up my barriers, I barely touched the surface and forced my way through the blood sacrifice without letting the scene draw me in. Heart galloping, I closed my eyes.

Darkness. Lots of darkness. Eons of darkness.

Had the object been buried? Lost from that early civilization, or hidden away? I lowered my shields and touched the pot again.

Blinding light. Flashes of color. Hands. Stories.

Darkness. Light.

But no Magician.

Then the light changed, and I recognized my valley. Even a thousand years ago, the light had the same blinding intensity, the same transparent, yellow-gold color.

This was the part the Magician needed me to see. This was his time. I relaxed my barriers and grasped the pot more firmly.

The walls of Ruined City reflected the golden morning light, but in this vision's time, the city was filled with people and life. The huge structure rose from the banks of the river to near the top of the red-walled cliff. An Anasazi settlement.

Intact, beautiful, safe.

Women sat on rooftops, grinding corn. A man climbed a lashed ladder, bringing home his share of the hunt.

Then I saw him and my pulse jumped in my chest like a rabbit in a snare. The Magician held the pot in his hands. He was an old man now, his hair almost silver, his hands gnarled.

A fire burned behind him, but not with intense heat. Just a campfire. He mixed herbs into the pot, whispered a blessing, and offered the noxious-smelling pot of steaming herbs to an old woman who lay on a pallet nearby.

Healing? The Magician used the pot for healing? Was this what I needed to learn now?

The Magician looked up at me, his eyes the same amber color as mine. Then the vision faded.

I flopped back on my pillow, exhausted but excited. I had to tell Forrest what I saw. I stowed the pot and ran most of the way to the sheriff's office. She'd be finished with work in less than an hour.

I'd stopped breathing hard by the time she came out the front entrance of the department's one-story building.

"Hey," Forrest called with a surprised grin. She waved good-bye to one of the deputies and hurried down the steps to give me a peck on the cheek "You look awful."

"Thanks." Guess I was a little sweaty.

I pulled her through the parking lot, away from the tourists who were walking by and noticing us a little too much. I swallowed through the stifling lump in my throat. "I tried another vision," I whispered.

49

She grimaced and took hold of my hands. "You should have waited for me. Please, Josh. Don't get lost in those awful scenes. I get so scared for you."

"No. It was fine this time. When I saw the Magician, I knew I'd gotten past the bad part."

I told her what I saw. The city. The Magician healing the old woman. Forrest let out a low whistle. "What do you think it means?"

By this point we were side by side, leaning on Tilley's bumper. I shrugged. "Hell if I know."

She flashed me a quick glance.

"Heck, I mean heck."

"You said one time you might be a healer for the tribe. Do you think that's what the Magician is trying to say?"

"Not much call for witch doctors anymore, even in a tribal setting."

She smiled at my attempt at a joke, but then grew serious again. "Maybe you're supposed to become a real doctor."

I rubbed my chin with the palm of my hand. "If that's the case, I better study harder for my chemistry test."

She nudged me with one hand, and I pretended to fall over to break the tension between us.

"Doctors have to go to college and medical school and do internships," she continued, listing the steps on her fingertips.

"Can't do that around here."

"Probably not." A cold, lonely feeling washed through me, and I didn't want to talk about the vision or its meaning anymore.

Forrest dug in her pocket for her keys, but the

expression on her face made my heart sink even deeper into my gut.

"Let's not interpret this too literally." I folded her hand into mine. "We have a long way to go before we know what the Magician really wants."

She studied my face intently. If we didn't have a solemn pact that she wouldn't read my thoughts, I'd swear she knew exactly what I was thinking.

Then she smiled, that beautiful, all-teeth-and-happiness-smile, and my heart glowed with the look she gave me. "You'll make a wonderful doctor."

I grinned at my feet and my cheeks and ears heated. Dr. Joshua Kwail. It did have a nice sound. And I did like chemistry, but it couldn't be the only message the Magician wanted to convey.

CHAPTER 6

The singer in the Friday night band at Hamburger Heaven crooned a slow, romantic song while I savored the last bite of cheesecake left on my plate. The sugar and fat and chocolate played on my tongue and drove my taste buds straight to stratospheric bliss.

Josh watched me from across the table and snickered. "You look like you've found nirvana."

I licked my fork and set it down with a sigh. "Close."

"Ready to head home?"

My pulse gave a quick jump. I had something I needed to tell Josh, to explain, and we needed to be alone when I did. "I should burn off a few of these yummy calories, so let's go for a walk first."

With a wave to our friends in the band, we left the rowdy commotion of the burger joint and walked down the street to the park. The night was quiet, no wind. The moon glowed behind thin, flowing clouds.

I let out a little sigh. Soon the tourists would be returning in droves, filling up the hotels and restaurants, but tonight the little ghost town was ours. I drew in a long, deep breath of mountain air to calm my apprehension.

"There'll be frost by morning." Josh took my hand as we climbed the steep steps to the park.

I could feel it too. The sharp, clear cold that sends the last of the green leaves to autumn color. We sat on the two swings in the park, and the chains squeaked when we pushed back and let ourselves fly.

Usually I love the motion of swinging. It tickles my stomach, and reminds me of being on a boat. I would stretch my toes to the sky and laugh out loud, but tonight I remained silent, staring up at the crescent moon.

Josh seemed to sense my need for quiet and waited for me to continue.

"I've been doing some research," I finally began.

He didn't say anything, but watched me as we swung in unison.

"You know I've always been interested in the flute you have. The one the Magician gave you the day we met."

He was listening carefully. I could tell by the way his head was tipped in my direction.

"It's a courting flute," he said quietly.

"Yes. I know." I slowed my motion. "But I couldn't find any information indicating the tribes around here used or believed in such a thing, and I looked everywhere. There are flutes for ceremonies, but not for…you know…romance or courting."

He glanced up, his eyes round. "George knew right away what the flute was used for."

"Yes, but he knows about the customs of lots of different tribes. He sells things at the Trading Post from many tribes, not just Hopi and Apache, and Yavapai."

"True."

"So, anyway, a courting flute was mostly used by the Plains peoples," I continued. I read three books on the subject, and searched online several times, and I was pretty sure I was on to something here, but I wanted Josh to make the connection…if there was one.

"Like the Lakota, or the Comanche?" He skidded to a stop.

I dragged my feet too. "I found a courting flute in lots of Lakota stories and legends. It sure looks like the strongest possibility, although customs get shared around among different tribes."

Josh was quiet for a while longer. Then he stood. I watched the knowledge dawning in his expression, but he hadn't looked at me yet. I let the understanding simmer for another while. Let him think it through to the end, just as I had. I stood quietly beside him, waiting for him to speak.

He rubbed one hand over his face and pushed back his hair. So cute. He needed a haircut. I would love to curl my fingers into the dark softness, but he was still concentrating, so I kept my hands to myself.

"The Lakota didn't move onto the plains until after the Magician lived here. Early on, they lived in the Midwest." He finally looked at me.

"The flute could be from an earlier civilization. Maybe the Lakota borrowed the tradition?" I suggested.

"Could be."

His thoughts were coming together, and my pulse raced, warming my cold cheeks.

"So, if the flute is from an ancient civilization to the north, and the pot is from an even older civilization to the south, then…"

I couldn't help myself. "Where did the necklace come from?" I blurted.

He gave an awkward shrug.

"Do you think they were always his things?" I asked, still a little breathless.

"He might have traded with other tribes. I'm sure some of the things in his burial site are trade items. He was a very wealthy, powerful man in his lifetime."

"So why did he give you only *those* things from his grave? Why do they hold such…"

"Magic?"

"Yeah, magic. And power."

He chewed on his lip for a moment. "And the even bigger question is, where did the Magician come from?"

The winter wind blew up the mountain and chilled me. I didn't know why, but deep inside I was scared.

****

Saturday afternoon, George had a Tribal Council meeting and left me in charge of the Trading Post. I had a busy afternoon. A busload of school kids from Phoenix wiped out our supply of fake arrowheads and plastic bows and arrows. And they didn't break anything, so the afternoon was profitable. George would be pleased.

I was wiping the grubby fingerprints off the glass counters and getting ready to close up when the bell on the front door rang. I glanced up. One more customer. Then I could go make a ham and cheese and pickle sandwich. My stomach had been rumbling for the past half hour.

I smiled at the woman, and she returned my smile. She was thin, tall, almost gaunt. Her long face showed deep lines of worry. Her hair had once been brown, but had faded to a dull gray. She wore it short, choppy, like she'd cut it herself.

Her eyes were a startling blue and drew my attention. Something bothered me about her eyes.

Her movements were jerky and awkward as she approached the counter. Her eyes never stopped moving as she searched the empty store, as if she expected someone to jump out and shout, "Boo!"

"Can I help you?" I asked. I really didn't expect she would rob me, but I edged closer to the panic button hidden beside the phone.

She stopped very close to the counter, glanced around once more, and dropped her chin. "Are you Josh?" Her voice whispered fear and signaled trouble.

My breath stopped short, and I frowned. How did she know my name?

I must have looked worried, because she held up her hand. "Please. My name is Angela, and I need your help."

****

Hiding a secret from Forrest is never easy, especially one this huge. We had already planned to hang out Sunday afternoon at Newspaper Rock, before meeting George in Prescott for dinner, but my heart banged in my chest all the way to the secret rendezvous at a desert ranch.

I distracted Forrest by talking about the cross-country team's road trip to Flag. She'd never been to the Grand Canyon, and chattered excitedly about seeing the national park for the first time.

She let me drive Tilley, and when we pulled up to the entrance, Forrest hopped out and pushed the rusty gate out of the way. I drove through. She dragged the dilapidated barrier back to the post, looped the chain over, and then jumped into Tilley's passenger seat with a grin on her pretty face.

I didn't have to drive too far up the dusty road.

Newspaper Rock is on private land, but the owner has always allowed my people to worship here.

My heart squeezed tighter in my chest. Our lives, especially Forrest's, were about to change. I hoped like hell—I mean heck—it would be for the better.

"Totally cool," Forrest wandered around the huge rock, studying the petroglyphs. "What do they mean?"

Trying to appear casual, I crossed my leg and leaned against the rickety park bench nearby. "Some are directions. Long ago, this was a crossroads for the people of the Southwest," I said. "Others are illustrations for stories. Who knows? Some could be ancient graffiti."

She chuckled. "Like 'Kilroy was here' from the 1200s."

"Kinda. This place has been a meeting place for centuries. People would gather here…" I surveyed the desert and spotted the woman lurking behind a mesquite tree not far from where we stood. I tried to keep my voice steady, even though my pulse raced and heat rose up my neck to my ears.

Forrest knelt down and traced a coyote design on the ancient boulder covered by thousands of petroglyphs.

"It's holy, isn't it?" she asked. "Do you come here often?"

"I usually visit with George. It's part of our tradition."

The woman stepped out from her hiding place.

Should I stay or go? I must have looked torn, because when Forrest glanced at me, she straightened and crossed her arms. "What's up, Josh?"

So busted. "Uh…There's someone you need to

meet."

Forrest shielded her eyes and studied the desert toward the river canyon to the north. "Is Zalo coming today?"

"No. I am." The woman moved forward a few more steps. "Forrest, honey. You probably don't remember me...."

When Forrest turned toward the stranger, her whole body tensed. Her hands made fists. She squinted her eyes and took a hesitant step forward. "Mom?"

The woman nodded and blinked back tears. That's what I'd recognized before. Forrest and her mom had the same blue-green eyes.

With a shout, Forrest flew into her mother's arms. The woman held on to her, both of them laughing and hugging and crying. My eyes stung, too. I dug my hands in my pockets and stared at my shoes.

Sure, I was happy for Forrest. Totally happy. So why had my throat tightened with pain? I dropped my gaze to give them a minute.

"You shouldn't have come," Forrest finally whispered to the woman. "It's too dangerous. What if you're caught? Or killed?"

Totally confused now, I stared at them.

"Josh? You knew about this?" Forrest shook my arm and drew me close. "You knew my mother was here? And you kept the secret?"

"Wasn't easy," I admitted.

"I came last night," Angela explained. "I couldn't take the chance anyone would see us together when we met, so Josh helped me."

"How'd you get away?"

Angela smiled and brushed Forrest's hair back

from her face. "I have so much to tell you. So much to explain, but I don't have much time."

I pointed to a rusted park bench nearby and turned to leave, but Angela put up a hand. "Wait, Josh. You need to know the truth too. I've watched the two of you together this week."

"All week?" Forrest squeaked.

"I had to know who is important to you now. I didn't want to worry your Gran, so a little spying was the next best thing. Sorry, sweetie."

Forrest took her mother's hand. "I get it."

****

My mother. Ho-ly shit. My mother was *here.* My heart kept thumping, and my chest hurt with the pressure. Happy pressure, like it would bust open with joy. No way would I get my breathing back to anything close to normal.

My mother was sitting next to me, holding my hand. I still couldn't believe it. How long had I dreamed of this day?

"Are you safe now?" I finally managed to choke out. "Can you come back from witness protection? Can you…."

Mom held up a hand to slow my questions, but I shook my head with impatience. Would she stay with me? Would she be my mother again?

"Let me explain everything. Then you can ask all the questions you want. No more lies, Forrest. That much I promise you."

My stomach took a tumble. "Lies?"

Mom dropped her chin and glanced away. She drew in a deep breath, like she was going to say something totally horrible. I waited, more freaked out

59

than ever. Did I even want to hear what she had to say?

"I wasn't in witness protection," she began.

"But Gran…"

"I made a deal with the FBI."

"Okay…then where have you been for the last, twelve…no, almost thirteen years?" I didn't hide the anger in my voice.

My mother heard it and flinched. "I've been in jail."

My turn to flinch.

"Please, honey," Mom pleaded. "Let me tell you the whole story."

I nodded and rubbed my numb arms. The desert moved in and out of my vision like a bad dream, so I focused on Josh. He hadn't said a word, just sat cross-legged on the ground nearby, drawing small figures in the sand with a stick, but he was listening carefully. I could tell by the set of his shoulders and the tilt of his head. I felt a little braver, knowing he was close to me.

Mom stood and paced a few times around the bench. The soft crunch of gravel filled the silence between us. She sat down next to me, close enough for me to catch her mom-scent. Funny how I'd never forgotten that subtle smell, though now it was partially masked by the reek of her fear.

Visibly shaking, Mom gulped a breath, swallowed, and steadied her shoulders. "Your grandmother has told you the story about how I loved the environment and tried to protect the forests of California."

It was painful, but I looked into her face.

"Your father and I worked to bring changes to the laws. To make people aware of the price we would pay if the old growth forests were destroyed, and the land

and rivers ruined."

Mom tried again to draw a breath, but her breath hitched. She laid her icy hand on mine. "There was a man we thought was a friend, a powerful, well-connected man. For now I'll call him Mr. Jones."

She blinked away a tear. "We thought he was helping us. He was very clever and very rich, but after a while, I grew suspicious of his motives. I tried to warn your father and the others who worked with us, but no one would listen. I knew because…"

"You can read people, too. Read the lies?"

"Yes." Mom searched my face and then smiled with her mouth and her eyes. "I'm so glad you understand…that you share the gift. This would be much harder to explain otherwise." Mom glanced at Josh with furrowed brows.

"It's all right." I said. "Josh knows everything. He understands."

"Okay." Mom squeezed my trembling hands with hers.

I didn't pull away.

"Jones used our group to gain control of the land for himself," Mom continued with more confidence in her tone. "He didn't want to save the spotted owl, or the old redwoods, but I hadn't figured out his true motivation. I still haven't."

"He grew suspicious and tried to push me out, but I was stubborn." She pinched her mouth into a tight frown and the lines on her face furrowed. "And stupid. I needed to know what he was up to, but I didn't know who to trust."

"Dad?"

"Your father laughed when I told him." Mom let

out a long, broken sigh. "Your father was a brilliant, caring man, but he never could see past the surface of what people were. I can't blame him. Jones is quite the con artist, a brilliant liar and he cared—no, cares—for no one but himself."

"A sociopath," Josh contributed.

"Yes. And evil."

"The man used your father to frame me for a serious crime."

"Did Dad realize what was going on?"

Mom blinked back the tears in her eyes, and I fought the sting in my own. "Not until it was too late. He was conned, just like the cops and the FBI."

"Did you tell the FBI?"

Mom bit her lip and stared at me for a long moment.

I shrugged. "I get it, tough to make them believe you."

"I had no proof. No alibi. I was trapped, so I made a deal. I would go to jail…"

"Jail?"

"I agreed to forgo a trial and plead guilty if the authorities would keep the story out of the press. I had to protect you. I lied to Gran, told her I was in protective custody." She dropped her chin. "It was sort of the truth."

My brain swirled, and I gulped to swallow the horrible taste in my mouth. I waded through the mind-churning information my mother had just dropped on me like a fifty-ton nuke. Everything I thought I knew about my family was a lie. Everything.

"So when did they release you?" I finally choked out.

Mom squeezed my hand again and gazed out across the dessert. "They didn't."

Josh glanced up, and his expression flashed from surprise to concern. "You escaped?"

"I had to," Mom said to both of us.

"Why?"

"Because he's here." Mom hissed, then glanced around nervously and rose from the bench. "I need to leave. Even this place is too exposed."

We headed toward the small gravel lot where we'd parked Tilley. Mom's arm rested on my shoulder, and I gave her a hug.

She was my mom. I loved her. No matter what she'd done, we'd figure it out. "Maybe we can help," I suggested as we neared my jeep.

"It's dangerous, Forrest. This man will do anything to get what he wants. Fortunately, Gran used her maiden name when she moved you here. I don't think he knows who you are yet. We need to keep you both safe."

"We're good at solving mysteries," Josh offered.

"I heard," Mom said with a brief smile.

"And we can move around without anyone suspecting us," I added.

"I need to stop this man. I can't let him get away with what he did to…"

"To…?" I asked.

Mom took hold of my shoulders and turned me so we were face-to-face. The pain in her eyes overwhelmed me, and I started to well up again.

"Your father." She barely whispered the words.

I stood very still for a long time, waiting. Hoping what I was thinking wasn't the truth. Hoping I was totally wrong. Hoping I was out in the cliché of left field with this crazy, horrible I-can't-believe-it thought. My heart twisted with pain and sorrow and grief. "Dad? He didn't run off and leave us."

"No."

"He's dead?" I whispered the gut-wrenching words.

"I'm sorry, darling."

I fought back tears for a man I hardly remembered. Big hands, a deep voice. A piggyback ride. I'd resented his absence my whole life. Cursed him more than a few times for leaving Gran and me to fend for ourselves. But he hadn't left us. He'd been stolen.

Josh hovered beside me. He rubbed my shoulder, and I leaned closer to him, grateful for his steady warmth.

Mom brushed the tears off my cheeks and kissed me. They both held me until I stopped crying and mopped up.

Josh was the first to speak. "This Jones killed him and framed you for your husband's murder."

Mom didn't deny it, and I understood the awful truth.

"Before your father was killed, I did try to get away. Get us all away. When I realized Jones had gone far beyond what I could stomach, and there was nothing I could do to stop him, I argued with your dad. I wanted to leave. He wouldn't, so I left on my own. I took you and ran. Gran helped me hide. Your father was killed the next night. He died alone."

I closed my eyes. "The cops found us. We were living near the beach."

"You remember?"

"Just flashes. You were building a sand castle for me, and a man came. You cried when he took you away."

"That day the police arrested me for your father's murder."

I was breathing hard, my arms rigid at my sides. I shook my head. "You should have fought the charges."

Mom gave me a quick, but gentle shake. "I was going to, Forrest, but more was at stake than my freedom. You. Your Gran. This man would have killed us all. I had to find a way to make him feel safe. It was the only way to keep you safe."

"So Gran took me and moved. And you went to jail."

"I always knew where you were." Mom gulped a couple of deep breaths, as if a huge load had been lifted off her thin shoulders. She turned to me, smiling. "I did my best."

****

My mother drove off in the beater car she'd hidden behind the old ranch shed. The dust from her tires swirled in the afternoon dust-devils.

"It's a lot to take in," I said to Josh.

"I get it." He tucked me in Tilley's passenger seat, took the keys from my hand, and drove slowly down the gravel road toward the highway entrance.

Good thing he knew how to drive. After everything Mom told me, I didn't have the strength to hold onto the steering wheel, or use the clutch to shift gears. My arms felt shaky, my knees wobbly. I tried to breathe deeply, but couldn't fill my lungs with enough air. I pushed my bangs out of my eyes and stared out Tilley's dinged-up windshield at the yellow-gold of the afternoon sunlight. A buzzy feeling of shock and regret wash over me.

Wind blew through the jeep, the air cool and fresh. I put my arm out the window and played airplane with my hand to distract my thoughts from the way-too-painful truths I just learned.

I finally found the words and spit them out. "My dad's dead."

"Yeah." Josh glanced at me and turned back to watch the road. "But your mom's here now."

"I'm afraid for her. The cops'll be after her. They're bound to figure out where she's hiding."

Josh's face brightened. "I know a place she could hide."

"Where?"

"With Zalo."

I turned to face him, let out an almost happy chuckle, and shook his arm. "Positively brilliant, Colonel Mustard."

"Why thank you, Miss Scarlet."

CHAPTER 7

I met Forrest after school on Tuesday. We had twenty minutes before track practice, so we hung out next to Tilley in the parking lot, the only place we could be alone anymore.

"I left Zalo a note with his Sunday biscuits," I said, after chugging a bottle of water. It was blazing hot again today, and we stood in the half shade of a paloverde tree. "And he's up for having company."

"Cool." Forrest dropped her pack in jeep's back seat and twisted open the water I offered her.

I stroked my hand through her long, I-can't-get-enough-of-it hair. She smiled at my touch, and I gave her a quick kiss. Then another. My heart was beating so hard I didn't hear Ms. Whipple walk by on the way to her car. A polite throat-clearing had us both jumping back, even though my English teacher pretended to ignore us.

Forrest snickered and then snuggled under my arm. "Mom showed up at the Connor hotel last night when I was working. You should have seen the disguise." She rolled her eyes and took another sip. "Ditzy blond wig, gobs of blue eye shadow. Ugh."

"But effective?"

"I suppose. We're planning to leave coded messages on the bulletin board at the hotel."

"We have track practice on Saturday, but we could hike in with her early Sunday morning. Let's meet at

67

the trailhead at dawn."

Forrest nodded, but then huffed a short raspberry through her lips. "I bugged Mom again about who this Jones guy really is, the creep she's so afraid of. She still won't tell me."

"She's protecting you."

"I know, I know. But if she's hiding at the Ruined City, how's she going to stop this guy? Maybe we could help her?"

"Might be a tough sell. You were pretty young when she left."

"Three, maybe four."

"She probably still thinks of you as a little kid. Someone to protect."

Forrest glanced up. "Will you talk to her?"

"Me?"

"Yeah. She trusts you."

I shook my head, but Forrest grabbed my arm.

"Convince her we can investigate without getting caught. This guy, whoever he is, will never suspect a couple of dopey teens." She did her hair-twisting, fake-blank look to demonstrate.

I laughed, but I wasn't sure her plan was a good idea. I was about to say so when Forrest landed a huge kiss on me. For a moment, I couldn't think of anything but how wonderful she felt in my arms.

"Wow," Forrest sighed after she relaxed on my chest after the kiss. Her breath tickled my neck, and I caught a whiff of her perfume. My head spun like an out-of-control Ferris wheel.

Pulling her closer, I tingled all over with need. I tightened my arms around her waist, and when she stood on tiptoe, our hearts beat together in a rhythm that was tougher and tougher for us to ignore.

"M-m-m," I hummed between kisses.

"We'd better get to practice," she whispered while nibbling on my ear.

"Damn."

She looked up at me. "What?"

I grinned at her, but took her hand and headed for the track. "I was hoping for another kiss."

She smiled her secret smile. "Later."

I followed her toward the field. Eventually the blood would return to my brain.

****

Sunrise on Sunday morning. I parked Tilley off road behind a dilapidated shed and hiked the rest of the way to the trailhead. I fibbed to Gran, making up a story about having an early call at the police station, so I could be here to meet Mom.

Did I feel guilty? Maybe just a bit, but helping my mother was more important than the truth.

Next to the trail marker, I found Josh's pack dumped in the dirt. I spotted him sitting with crossed legs on a rocky shelf nearby. Perfectly still, he faced the rising sun. He reminded me of a statue I'd seen at a Buddist temple back in California. The morning sun glowed in an aura around him.

I unhitched my loaded backpack and silently climbed to his side.

"Hey," he said without opening his eyes.

"How's the spirit world?"

"Wouldn't know. I felt cold sitting in the shade, so I moved up here. Ever notice how the sunlight can go right through your eyelids?"

I sat next to him, knee to knee, and copied his pose.

After a few moments of deep breathing, a peaceful golden flow moved through me, and I felt more relaxed than I had in weeks.

Then a chuckle rippled out from below. "Hello-o-o, my young Buddhas."

"Morning, Mom," I called happily, and jumped down from the rock to give her a huge hug.

"Sorry I'm late," she said a little breathlessly as she unloaded her pack. "I hid the car a few miles back and walked the rest of the way."

Josh jumped down from the rocks and joined us. "Good idea."

"I wiped it down for fingerprints and buried the license plate."

I nudged Josh and tipped my chin his way. "Ask her," I hissed in his ear.

Mom glanced between us. "Ask me what?"

"Forrest wants us to…help," Josh said, "with your investigation."

I threw my hands in the air. "Oh, very convincing, Kwail."

"Sorry," he wheedled with a shrug. "I'm not sure we can do much without getting everyone in a heck of a lot more trouble."

"So my mom's supposed to sit in a mud hut and wait while we ignore the fact that a major injustice has taken place. My father was murdered." My voice had pitched higher, louder. "I think…"

Mom raised a hand to interrupt our argument. "Forrest…"

I rounded on her. "What?"

"I'm not going to hide in a mud hut. I have a plan." She paused for a mega-moment. "And there is something you can do."

I stopped breathing and waited.

Mom leaned against the wooden trail sign and pressed her lips together. I didn't try to read her thoughts, but I could feel the debate going on in her mind.

"I've learned more this week," she continued. "I'm closer to understanding at least some of 'Jones's' plan, and I do need your help."

Excitement rippled through me. "Anything."

She took me by the shoulders and leveled her blue-green eyes at mine. "I need you to take your Gran and leave Arizona."

"What?" My heart tightened into a pounding fist. "Run away?"

"Yes. As far as you can."

Josh took a step back, and I threw him an evil look. Wise move, buddy. Stuff was gonna 'splode.

"We can move Gran somewhere," I said through clenched teeth, "if you think it's best."

Mom let out a sigh, but then I crossed my arms and stuck out my jaw "I'm not going anywhere," I enunciated slowly. I know, I know. I sounded like an angry two-year-old, but who the heck cared? At least I didn't stamp my foot. No way was I going to ditch my mother now she was finally back in my life.

Mom pushed her hair back from her face and glanced at Josh. He shot her an I-can't-help-you shrug, and she let out a long sigh. "Forrest, I understand. In your position, I probably wouldn't budge either. But I have to warn you," she put up a mom finger and wagged it at both of us. "You have no idea how powerful...how evil, this man is. I've spent the past fourteen years watching him."

"Mom, please let us help."

Although she looked even more doubtful, she shook her head and said, "I'll think about it."

****

Moving Mom into the Ruined City was a cinch. After we hiked downstream, Zalo greeted her and showed her the warm, safe room he'd prepared.

Hilarious. He acted like he was the proud owner of a fancy French chateau, not a thousand-year-old, broken-down Anasazi ruin.

Her space was lower on the cliff than his room, and it was easy for her to climb the few steps to the entrance. The roof and walls appeared solid, and the dirt floor was dry and swept clean. He'd foraged a nice blanket from somewhere, and even a pillow for the straw bed.

"It's lovely, Zalo. Thank you." Mom glanced around happily. "And I love the view. I feel like I'm staying at a five-star hotel."

Zalo blushed and toed the dirt floor.

"I hear you know lots of native legends," Mom continued.

That was all it took. Total bonding. The two climbed down the cliff, settled by the small fire creek side, and started talking. Mostly Zalo talked and Mom listened.

Josh and I unloaded the supplies we'd carried in, and searched for some extra firewood. They'd need the extra fuel, with the nights growing longer and colder.

After Josh dropped another load of logs on the pile, he brushed off his hands on the back of his jeans. "If you need anything, Zalo, leave a note at the shop under that old picture of me, The one on the bulletin board."

"Got it." Zalo put out his hand to shake Josh's.

"And if you run out of food…" I added.

"Stop worrying, Forrest. We'll be fine." Mom chuckled. "I'm used to rougher conditions than this. Zalo and I will keep each other company."

"Anything else?" I still hoped she'd relent and involve us in her sleuthing.

"Yes," Mom hesitated and then took my hands. "There's one more thing, but you have to be very careful. You can't mention it to anyone."

My heart bumped up in speed, and I forced my feet not to jump up and down like a little kid waiting for her ice cream. "Sure," I said with fake adult calm.

She turned to Josh. "Not even your cousin?"

Josh hitched one shoulder to signal his agreement.

I held my breath. Did she really trust us enough to help with the investigation?

"Would you two go to Sedona sometime soon? I need a map of the vortexes in that area."

"Okay, but what…?"

Mom interrupted. "You can find one at the Chamber of Commerce." She chuckled lightly. "I hear vortexes are a big draw for the tourists here."

I opened my mouth again, but she gently touched her finger to my lips to silence me.

"I'll tell you more when I have the problem worked out. Promise. Having a good map would be a huge help."

Swamped with curiosity, I nodded, and she kissed my cheek. It was a start.

"Thanks," she said. "I know you want to help."

****

73

School dragged on all week. No messages from Mom or Zalo. No appearances from Josh's spook either.

I drove down to Verde early Saturday morning, so glad for the weekend that I wanted to shout.

"Sedona?" Josh jumped in the passenger seat and rubbed his hands together.

"Easier to search for the maps online," I suggested.

With a shake of his head, he buckled his seatbelt. "Your mom was pretty specific. She wants us to go to the Chamber of Commerce to get that particular map."

I started Tilley. It took a couple of hours to drive to Sedona, but whatever. I just hoped this wasn't Mom's grand plan to keep us out of her way.

"You think she's giving you busywork?"

I pulled out onto the quiet road. "What gave me away?

He touched my cheek lightly. "That frown on your face."

We arrived in the tourist town in great time, and Josh had only cringed once. Well…twice. I guess he was getting used to my good driving, because he hardly ever yelled anymore.

I gritted my teeth and only honked twice at the Saturday morning backup. Pretty good for me. Snowbirds drive so-o slowly. The late October day was mild. I tried to be patient with the traffic along the main drag in Sedona, and finally parked Tilley on a side street.

Saturday's the busiest day in any small tourist town, and Sedona was no different. Cars and people choked the roads and sidewalks, but before long we found the Chamber of Commerce office, right next to a rowdy cowboy bar. An off-key western love song slurped onto the fake wooden sidewalks. Josh sang the refrain, and I laughed at his yodel.

He opened the door for me, and we entered the heavily air-conditioned room. Goose bumps from the cold air rippled up my arms.

Shelves filled with maps and tour information lined the walls of the small storefront. Speaking in loud, slow English, a teenage volunteer was pointing out tourist sites to a German couple.

An older man looked up from the long counter, tipped back his Stetson and greeted us. "Kin I help ya?"

I glanced around and then smiled at him. "Do you have a map of the vortices?"

"*Shore do*," he replied with a two-ton western twang. He brushed two fingers through his bushy, grey mustache. "We call 'em vortexes 'round here. Do ya want the map of the hikin' trails too? Several of the most pow'ful vortexes can't be reached with your car."

I bit my lip to keep from chuckling. Was this guy for real? "Uh, sure."

He handed me two brightly printed brochures, but the maps were little more than sketches. "Anything else, little lady?"

"Do you have a topographical map?" It cost ten dollars, but I knew it would give Mom more detail. I handed over the cash.

Josh had wandered over to the side wall near the window. I bet he was trying not to laugh at the good ol' boy's had-to-be-fake accent. I headed across the room, but then noticed a crumpled flyer tacked to the public bulletin board, and a cold, itchy tingle slithered down my spine.

Partially hidden by an ad for the upcoming rodeo, only the top half of the poster was visible. I lifted the rodeo ad. The flyer had been mangled, and the bottom of the page was ripped away. Probably tossed after the election this summer.

A very handsome older man grinned out from the picture, and below, the remaining words read,

Vote for

Yavapai County.

Why was the poster still here months after the election? Even more important, why had I noticed it?

More cold blasted the base of my neck. I rubbed away the goose bumps, but the chill remained.

Pointing to the page, I asked Josh, "Do you know him?"

Josh leaned over, studied the picture, and shrugged. "Don't think so, but he's kinda sleazy."

Chewing on my lip, I stared at the man's picture a little longer. Expensive suit, perfectly knotted tie, full head of hair, only greying at the temples.

I walked around the room slowly, but nothing else in the space pulled the chill up my spine. Is this what Josh felt when he touched something?

I glanced toward the counter. The old guy was busy with a pair of leathered-up biker dudes, and the teen had disappeared into the back room. As I walked toward the door, I snatched the poster and grabbed Josh with my other hand. "Let's get out of here."

Josh followed me to the parking lot, silent the whole way. I was too busy with my own thoughts to notice his expression until I stopped to dig my keys out of the front pocket of my jeans.

His eyes were narrowed, his lips thinned. He

looked worried. A now-what-do-I do-about-my-crazy girlfriend worried. "Why'd you swipe that?"

I didn't understand myself, but I had to come up with something. I bit my lip to help me think, and then I knew. I held up the flyer. "Can you take a read on this?"

At first, Josh was surprised, but then he lowered his brows, and the corners of his mouth drooped. "I don't like to look, Forrest."

"I know. Believe me, I get it. But something isn't right, and I need your help. I don't have your gift."

He opened his mouth to object.

"Please?"

Letting out a long sigh, he rubbed a hand over his face. "Ooo-kay. But let's find a quiet place. If there's something to your suspicions, I don't want to do this in public."

We headed north, up Oak Creek Canyon. Near town, tons of tourists drove along the winding, forested road. The cottonwood trees and aspens filled the narrow canyon with a paint box of fall color. Their golden leaves, mixed with the pines and the red rock cliffs, made for gorgeous views.

Any other time, I would have loved the drive—all the tight curves on the road were a total blast, but my heart was thumping with heavy beats, and my knuckles ached with tension from my grip on the steering wheel. Finally the traffic thinned out.

A couple of miles past Slippery Rock, I parked Tilley at a roadside picnic area, and we walked down to the river. Aspen leaves rustled in the breeze, and the clear water of Oak Creek slid over polished red sandstone, bubbling with small waterfalls and eddies. A peaceful place, most of the time. But I was scared. No, terrified.

Josh hadn't said a word since we left Sedona.

I carried the poster. He'd need time to prepare before I handed over the page. We found a fallen log and sat together. No one else was nearby.

I sucked in a few deep breaths to settle my pulse. Asking Josh to use his gift was a huge favor. The readings were often frightening, sometimes painful. "I wouldn't …"

He held up a hand to interrupt me. "I know, Forrest. This is important. Just give me a minute." He closed his eyes, and I sensed the tension in his body, but also his spirit. Our elbows touching, I sat beside him, afraid to move. Afraid to even breathe.

"Okay, give it to me."

Forrest handed me the poster, and I closed my eyes again. I lowered my defenses slowly, not sure what to expect.

Hands. A bright room. Rock music from the seventies. Telephones ringing.

A handsome man in an expensive-looking suit straightened his George Bush tie and posed for a picture. A photographer adjusted the lighting, and a girl dusted powder onto the man's brow.

I waited. What was I supposed to see? Nothing seemed significant. Or threatening. Just a stupid campaign poster.

The man turned and stared at me. I sucked in a breath. How did he know I was watching?

A black force moved closer, and dark eyes stared into mine.

I couldn't....

Forrest called my name, but her voice seemed very far away. An echo more than a real sound.

My shields failed, and I braced myself for the onslaught.

A power took hold of me. Very old. Very black. I struggled to free myself, but couldn't move. Couldn't pull back from the blackness of the evil.

The specter said something in a deep, ominous tone. I understood the threat, although the words were not English. I shivered with cold, with terror. Within the control of the vision, my heart pounded in my chest with a sickening beat.

Then the Magician stepped between us.

"Stop." Forrest shook me by the shoulders.

I dropped the poster

"Josh, stop," she shouted again, digging her fingers into my arms.

After a long moment, I could open my eyes.

Her face was pale, frightened. Her blue-green eyes were wide and bright with tears.

I sucked in air, but it took all my strength to return myself back to the peacefulness of the river.

"Did you watch?" I choked out.

"Yes." She was gulping air and pulled me to her. "I thought I'd lost you. You wouldn't speak to me. You just kept saying this weird word I didn't understand." She repeated it.

I closed my eyes and held on to her. Finally I could speak. "It means danger."

When I could walk, Forrest helped me back to the parking lot. In the back seat, she found an old history binder to hide the poster. Touching the page again would be very dangerous. Definitely for me, maybe even for her.

I climbed into the jeep and leaned my head back on the seat, exhausted. No, it was more. The evil within the reading was still nearby, watching. I shivered and fought to free myself from his power. I called on my training and struggled to rebuild my defenses. I visualized my wall, building it stone by stone, until I could finally close off the powerful vision in the blackness.

Finally I could breathe. Finally I could think.

"It's him," Forrest said. Her teeth chattered, and she rubbed her arms like she was freezing. "The man who murdered my father."

"I think so." I studied her terrified expression. "Did you see the Magician?"

Her brows arched in surprise. "Was he there too?"

"He stopped the reading. Stood between me and...whatever, whoever that was. I don't understand why."

Forrest twisted her lips. "Maybe we're not strong enough to deal with the danger."

I rubbed my hands over my eyes and finally cleared my head completely. "I don't think we have a choice. Was that your Mom's plan? Did she want us to find the poster?"

Forrest found her keys. "Let's go ask her," she growled ominously.

I closed my eyes and held on. With the jeep's four-wheel power and Forrest's crazy, what-speed-limit? driving, we were at the trailhead of the Ruined City late that afternoon.

We hiked around the last bend in the river and waved. I didn't see Zalo, but Angela looked up. She was sitting by the fire.

She stood and brushed her hands over the back of her jeans. "I didn't expect you until tomorrow."

Forrest approached her mother. "This couldn't wait."

The frightened tone in Forrest's voice had Angela frowning. "What is it? What's wrong?"

"We have the vortex maps from Sedona, but that wasn't what you sent us to find, was it?" I was pissed. Where did the woman get off fucking with us? She'd promised Forrest. No more lies.

Angela glanced at me and then at Forrest. Her frown buckled her brow and deepened the lines around her mouth.

"Mom. Josh could've been hurt. We needed a warning. Time to prepare."

"I don't understand."

"Jones. We found him," Forrest shouted, waving the binder above her head. "The creep could have hurt Josh."

Angela drew a trembling hand through her hair. "Josh, I'm sorry. I never meant..."

My anger had cooled a little, and I shrugged one shoulder. "Forrest was the one who first noticed the poster."

Angela touched her daughter's arm. "Tell me what you felt." Her whispered tone sounded so frightened.

"Cold." Forrest closed her eyes and rubbed the back of her neck. "I shivered. So many lies. I've never known darkness like that before."

Angela swallowed carefully, but remained silent.

Forrest narrowed her eyes, seeming to look within her power. "I don't usually read things—objects. That

81

surprised me. Even a picture of the man's face was enough for me to sense the lies."

Angela chewed on her lip for a moment. "I had no idea. The campaign has been over for months. I knew he'd won."

I stood back and tried to believe her, but again, my gut twisted into cold, angry knots. "So this wasn't a test?" I ground out.

"No." She dodged my angry stare, so I didn't buy her bogus story.

Forrest glanced from me to her mother with a shocked expression. "Did he kill my father?" She whispered the words like others might be able to overhear.

"Yes." Angela moved slowly, like an old woman. She lowered herself to sit by the fire, folded her arms around her knees, and rocked back and forth.

Forrest sat beside her. "Mom, whoever this guy is, I don't think you can fight him alone. I don't think you're strong enough to stop him."

Angela stared up at the canyon walls above us. "I have to be."

****

I hunted for firewood while Forrest hiked downriver to find Zalo. Back in camp, I dumped the logs, brushed off my hands and stared at Angela. "How'd you know about me?" I demanded impatiently. "How'd you know about my gift? Did Forrest tell you? Or did you read my thoughts?"

Angela turned and studied my face. I gave her my best blank look, but she smiled. "You want to protect Forrest even more than you want to protect yourself. You love her, don't you?"

My neck and cheeks and even my ears burned with embarrassment and then anger. "It's not fair to pop into people's heads uninvited."

She laughed, but her tone didn't sound cruel. "Josh. I've been reading minds since I was twelve. I even did a street act in Vegas one year, when I was young and foolish. Of course, I had to pretend I was reading a lot of things I didn't really see, but every once in a while, I would zing my patsy with a deep-down truth."

I shoved my hands in my pockets. "Not very honest, if you ask me."

"Probably not." She returned to the fire and warmed her hands. "But I ate that summer, and there were times before when I didn't."

She studied me again, and I had no idea if she was reading me. *Armadillo,* I thought out of the blue.

"Armadillo?"

My turn to stare at her. "I didn't even feel you," I said, totally amazed.

She stirred the campfire, setting aside some glowing embers. "Can you tell when Forrest is reading you?"

"Almost always."

"That's because she's young and not as adept." She added another small log to the campfire. The sparks flew up and danced in the light breeze. "Don't misunderstand. Forrest has a very powerful gift, which will grow in strength as she matures, but you two are so connected." She let her eyes roam over me. "I've never met a person with psychometric skills before. I'm not sure, but I think your gifts are beginning to intertwine with Forrest's."

Zalo and Forrest appeared in the distance. Zalo

carried a string of nice-looking fish. Forrest had harvested a few wild onions from the river bank.

Angela watched her daughter. "She's a beauty."

"Yes."

She glanced over and waited for me to continue.

"And yes," I finally admitted, even to myself. "I do love her."

CHAPTER 8

We piled the fish tails and a stack of tiny bones on Zalo's one old cracked plate. Zalo rubbed his belly and smiled as he polished off the last of George's biscuits.

I glanced over at Forrest. "The sun'll set in the next hour. We should head back pretty soon."

She nodded and buckled on her day pack while I brushed the dry sand off my feet and put on my hiking boots.

"Do you have your phone, darling?" Angela asked.

"Sure." Forrest pulled out her fancy new gadget. "My old ratty one drowned in the flood."

"Do you have cell coverage here?"

"Think so." Waving her phone, she nodded. "Yep. Three bars."

"It's Saturday night. Why not call your Gran and ask her if you can stay overnight with a friend?" Angela took her daughter's hand. "I know, it's a small white lie, but I have so much to tell you. Now seems like the right time."

I glanced at Forrest and shrugged. "I can walk out alone."

"You both should stay, Josh," Angela added.

We nodded, and I sat back down in the warm sand. "Sure, but I'd better call George. He's been on a rampage since I got caught in that flood."

Forrest scooted over very close to her mother. "Does Gran know you're back?"

Angela shook her head.

"Don't you think she should? Maybe you could talk to her." Forrest offered her mother the phone.

"No. Not yet."

Forrest shot Angela a look of disappointment.

"Soon. I promise."

By the time we both called home and delivered our white lies, the fire had burned down to glowing embers. The evening was warm, so we didn't add any more logs. Better not to have a blazing fire after it got dark anyway. It might attract company, even as far out in the desert as we were.

Since Zalo caught the fish, and we cooked, Angela cleaned up dinner. I think she needed time to pull her thoughts together, but I didn't mind not having to scrub the plate with sand in the cold creek.

Forrest fidgeted next to me, so I moved closer and put an arm around her shoulders. She leaned toward me. I kissed her temple and smoothed my hand down her soft hair.

Zalo rolled his eyes and turned the other way. "Mushy," he said under his breath.

I turned and kissed her once more. She opened her mouth and playfully touched her tongue to my lips. My heart thumped more quickly, and the warm feeling of need spread through me. I pulled her closer to feel her heat, but Angela was stomping up the trail toward us, so we separated. Reluctantly.

Forrest cleared her throat.

"Are you ready?" Angela asked, studying each of us in turn.

"Maybe…" Zalo rose to leave.

"No, stay, dear. You're a part of this, too."

He settled onto his haunches, hands held close to the fire.

"Tell us about the creep," I said to start the conversation.

"He calls himself Laurence. Such an innocuous name, don't you think? Like some good ol' boy." With a brief sigh, Angela took a sip of water and chewed her lip for a moment. "He used the alias Howard Larson back when I knew him in Oregon. He disappeared from the Northwest shortly after he murdered your father, and it took me several years to track him down again."

"How?" Forrest jumped in. "Sorry. I mean, if you were in jail, how…"

"They have computers in jails. I had some IT training, so I offered to work in the tech lab and teach other inmates skills to use when they were released. I had time…."

Forrest let out a brief snort. "My mom the hacker."

Angela shrugged one shoulder and gave us a half smile. "Anyway," she continued, "our suspect has used at least two, maybe three other names over the past fourteen years. He didn't appear to be up to much more than running some simple scams, mostly low-key industrial espionage. You know, stealing secrets from one company to sell to another.

"Then a few years ago he got into hedge fund investing. He started a sham company and cheated a few investors, but he was pulling in a lot of money at the time, and I couldn't find the source. Spending a lot too, but I never could figure out what he was buying."

Angela twisted one hand with the other. "About two years ago, he disappeared for a couple of months, and then showed up here with a new alias. In less than a year, he got himself elected to Arizona's State House."

"Why?" I asked.

"Why what?" Angela focused on my face.

"Why here? Why go to through the effort of getting elected to the state congress?"

"I'm not sure yet." She rubbed her palm over her cheek and raked her fingers through her short hair.

Funny, Forrest did pretty much the same thing when she was worried about something important.

"But how does he walk into a new place and get himself elected?" I pressed her. "Doesn't that take time, connections?"

"For most people, yes. Laurence, as he's calling himself these days, is very smooth. Very glib. And extremely adept at using technology. And from what I can see, he invents his connections. Makes up a new life, new education, new career.

"Like witness protection?" Zalo put in.

"Only better," Angela said. "I've traced his new identity all the way back to his mythical grandparents. No one would ever know he's not the real Laurence Patterson, born 52 years ago in Winslow, Arizona. He has pictures, stories from friends. It's really quite amazing."

"But how?" I asked. There was more to Angela's story than this guy being a crooked hacker.

"If you have enough money, you can bribe people,

forge documents. Remember, he was doing industrial espionage in one of his last incarnations."

Forrest tapped one finger on her lip. "The question is...why does he want to be in the legislature?"

I agreed. "If he's as smart and diabolical as you think he is, then he has a good reason to choose such a public position."

"That's what I'm working on," Angela stared into the fire and a steely, I'm-going-to-get-the-creep-look flashed across her face. She glanced around the narrow canyon. "It has something to do with this place."

"The canyon?" I asked.

Angela threw out her hands and swept them back. "The whole area. This canyon, the valley, this part of Arizona. That's why I wanted a good map of the area."

Angela turned to me, and the firelight reflected in her eyes. "Now tell me, Josh. What did you see when you touched the poster?"

"Don't you already know?"

"Glimpses." She shook her head. "Tell me in your own words."

I looked Angela square in the face. "Well, I can tell you this. Your friend Laurence is old. Very powerful. And one really bad ass."

I related the rest of the story quickly. Forrest had carried the poster to the campsite in her pack, and we were both glad to hand it over to Angela.

The quarter moon rose over the top of the plateau and filled the canyon with eerie blue light. The sound of the flowing creek seemed closer, and a great horned owl flew overhead, flapping its huge wings as it searched for its next meal. I heard a sudden high squeal. Success for the owl meant death for some small creature.

I leaned back and stared at the dark sky a moment. "We need a plan."

"Yes," Angela agreed. "I'm working on one."

"Mom," interrupted Forrest. "We can help."

"No," Angel said vehemently. "I won't risk your lives." She took Forrest's hands in hers. "Please. You've done enough. I'm very grateful for the map and for Josh's information, but I need to do this alone." She squeezed Forrest's hands. "Promise me, both of you. You won't interfere."

Forrest sighed, but gave her mother a nod. I stared at the glowing embers of the fire.

Angela dismissed the subject with a wave of her hand and stood, glancing toward Forrest. "It's time for bed, Forrest. I have plenty of room for you."

Forrest flashed me a quick frown of disappointment.

"Josh," Angela continued, "you don't mind sleeping by the fire, do you? Zalo has an extra blanket."

I'd been hoping for some company, but wouldn't admit that out loud, especially to Angela. "Sure. Fine," I said, faking an upbeat attitude.

"Great." Angela dusted off her hands, turned, and headed up the hill.

Zalo had already climbed partway up the steep cliff to his shelter. Hand over hand, he scooted across a very narrow ledge to his room high on the cliff. "I'll toss ya down a blanket, bro," he said with an underlying chuckle in his voice.

"Thanks," I called up to him.

Angela glanced over her shoulder. "Take a minute to say goodnight," she said to Forrest with a smile.

When we stood, Forrest turned to me and wrapped her arms around my waist. She smelled of wood smoke and lavender shampoo, and she gazed up into my face, smiling. "Me too," she said under her breath.

"Me too, what?" I whispered into her ear as I nibbled the silky top edge. She shivered, and I pulled her closer.

"I wish we could both sleep by the fire." She let out a long sigh, and kneaded my back with her strong fingers

I kissed her gently and touched her cheek, drawing my thumb along the softness of her jaw. "We'll find the right place and the right time."

"For-rest," Angela called from above.

Forrest stood on her toes and gave me one more incredible kiss. I almost fell over when she drew back. "Good night."

A blanket plopped down on the sand nearby, and another chuckle rippled from above. "Good ni-i-ght," Zalo mimicked.

"Yeah, good night to you too." I threw the blanket over my shoulders and poked the fire with a little too much force. Sparks flew up into the night, and the owl called from somewhere down the canyon. We needed a plan, and I had plenty of time to dream one up.

****

I found Josh by the river in the morning. I climbed over a few boulders and sat beside him, but cringed and glanced away when he attached a worm to a fishhook. Gross.

"How'd you sleep?" he asked as he tossed the line in the quiet pool of deep water.

I shrugged. "Mom snores."

He grinned, but then reacted to a tug on the line. He landed an undersized trout, so he carefully removed the hook and let it go. The rainbow-sided fish splashed under the water and disappeared.

"I've been thinking," he said as he stared at the hook.

"Me too."

He shot me an amazing smile, and my heart gave a quick thump. "You have to know what a fish wants to eat before you prepare the hook to catch it."

I pushed back my hair. "And we don't know what our 'fish' wants, do we?"

"No."

"Someone needs to get close to our fish, maybe talk to him." Her voice rose with excitement. "He's a local politician. It shouldn't be too hard for someone to get in to see him."

"He's already knows me." Josh baited the hook with another worm. "He's seen me in the vision. Plus, the day you were lost in the flood, he came by to offer his 'condolences'."

I shielded my eyes and gazed into the distance. "Do you think he'd recognize me?"

"If you don't use your gift, I don't think so, but you need to go with someone else. Someone to protect you, just in case. Otherwise you'll end up so much owl meat."

"I'll go," Zalo stood on the edge of the creek. "I'll watch out for Forrest."

****

"Josh, wait." George leveled his dark eyes at me. It was early Monday morning, and I was late for the bus.

He crossed his arms in his Grand-Inquisitor way.

"What's up with the biscuits?" he said with a growl.

I squirmed but gave him my best totally innocent expression. "Biscuits? What do you mean?"

George held up the empty metal tray. "I mean, I left two dozen freshly baked biscuits on this tray last night, and now we have three."

"I was hungry in the middle of the night." I offered with a shrug, but my pulse started to race, and in a minute the tops of my ears would burn.

He grunted. "Not even you are that hungry."

I turned my back, pretending to rearrange my books inside my pack. Should I fess up? There'd been no problem when Zalo only foraged for one, but now two people were hiding in the canyon, and depending on George's baking skills.

Retreat seemed my best option. "I gotta go." I grabbed my track bag and was almost out the door when he said, "If he needs more to eat, let me know. Okay?"

I stopped and stared at the floor for a moment.

"I caught Zalo creeping in last night," George answered my unspoken question.

Man, so busted. I let out a groan

"At least he left us a few biscuits for breakfast." There was a trace of a chuckle in his comment. "Who else are you hiding?"

I grimaced, but turned to face him.

George waited. "It's not another kid, is it?"

I shook my head. "It's complicated."

"Are you in trouble?"

"No."

"Are they?"

"Kinda." I pushed out a breath. "I'll tell you as

soon as I can. Promise. As soon as it's safe…"

He walked slowly toward me, but then, to my surprise, he smiled and patted my shoulder. "Be careful, Josh. Let me know if you need help."

I nodded and dashed out the door. I had to run to catch the bus.

****

I turned up the electric fan and pulled my hair into a ponytail, but the small file room felt like Gran's oven when she was baking cookies.

I'd spent my entire after-school shift at the police station, buried in the hot, stuffy room. Near quitting time, Grady sent a message for me to come to her office before I took off for the evening. I smiled. Was I finally forgiven for conning the cops into taking me on that fateful ride-along?

I'd done nothing but file boring reports since the disaster at the river. Maybe now she'd let me start going on patrols and learn real cop stuff again.

I thought about my mom, the convicted murderer, and a shiver ran up my spine. What would Grady do if she knew I was sheltering a felon? I chewed my longest fingernail, counting the laws I was breaking. Would I ever earn a badge, or just a stint in jail for harboring a "dangerous" fugitive?

Near six o'clock, I stood in front of my commanding officer's door, but couldn't seem to work up the courage to knock. I squared my shoulders. *Grow up, girl.* Grady probably wanted to talk about scheduling my volunteer hours around track practices. I knocked on her door and peeked inside.

Grady scowled at me from behind her desk, and my heart took a dive in the dirt. Awesome. Now what?

93

"Come in, Forrest." With a fakey smile, she pointed to a chair opposite her desk. "Now don't look so worried. I just need to ask you a few questions."

I sat on the hard wooden chair and swallowed carefully, folding my hands in my lap. "About what?" No matter how nice her words sounded, Grady was still pissed, mouth pinched, eyes unsmiling, her shoulders stiff and pulled forward. Problem was, she'd notice if I dared read her now.

She fiddled with a piece of paper, set it down, and steepled her hands over it. She cleared her throat once, and then again.

I raised a brow in surprise. She was as nervous as I was.

"I've had a communication from the state police in northern California. They want to know if we've come across a fugitive they're searching for. They think this person might be heading to central Arizona. You and your Gran are the only new residents from California. Pescadero, right?"

My heart rattled in my chest, but I managed to keep my face calm, my eyes level. I nodded, but held my breath. I gave her my best innocent, bat-my-lashes look. "Who is he?"

Grady drummed her fingers on her desk. "She."

I was about to start twirling my hair when the door banged open, and I jumped at least a foot.

Manny Gutierrez filled the doorway and wore a seriously pissed-off face.

Grady glared at him. "Sergeant? This is a private meeting."

"Go home, Forrest," Manny ordered through clenched teeth.

Manny'd helped me and Josh in the past, and now used the title of sergeant to justify hanging around the department. Special Agent caused too many raised eyebrows.

"What business…?" Grady sputtered, then stood and jutted her jaw. "I need to speak with my intern."

"You're interviewing a minor without a parent present? Without a lawyer?"

Grady blanched. "Forrest volunteers here. This is not in any way an official—"

He leaned over Grady's desk and hissed, "You're being used."

With supreme calm, Grady turned to me. "Go on home, Forrest. I'm sorry. Despite what the sergeant says, I didn't mean to upset you."

I scooted past Manny and out the door as fast as I could. I ran down the hall and hid in the bathroom for a moment to catch my breath. I'd call Josh as soon as I got out of here. I laid the back of my head against the door. How had Manny known about the meeting? And did he know about my mom?

I heard footsteps, then Manny's voice. I didn't understand why, but he and Grady must be heading to the conference room at the end of the hall. Carefully, silently, I opened the bathroom door a crack to hear what they were saying.

Yeah, I know. Gran's always ragging on me for eavesdropping, but no adult ever tells the truth, so what choice did I have?

"We can talk down here." Manny still sounded totally pissed off.

He had Grady by the arm, but she pulled away. "I wasn't doing anything unethical, Sergeant," she whispered angrily. "You've got this all wrong."

He rested his hands on his duty belt. "Where'd you get the tip about the fugitive?"

Silence for a moment. "The notice came in this morning's communications from someplace in northern California. Don't remember the town offhand. Someplace up north."

"Did you call their office? Contact the officer in charge of the investigation?"

"No, but I would have...after..." She rubbed her forehead. "Damn thing looked official."

Manny grunted. "And it named Forrest?"

"Not exactly. They asked about anyone who'd moved here from northern California who might have had contact—"

"Have you had your office swept for bugs lately?"

"Are you kidding?" Grady fisted her hands on her hips and laughed. "Who would bug my office? That's ridiculous."

Manny steamed out a breath. He took Grady by the arm, but more gently this time. She flashed him a look that was wa-a-ay more than professional courtesy.

Whoa. More mysteries. I raised a hand, but missed what they were thinking because Manny closed the door to the conference room.

I blew out a breath, turned, and leaned my forehead against the cool tile. I didn't need a mind-read to sense the attraction between them. Lust hung in the air like a pheromone fog. Question was...did they even know it themselves?

The even bigger question had my stomach in a free fall. Who had sent in the tip, and what did they know about my mother?

CHAPTER 9

Josh flipped out when I called him. "Is Grady going to arrest you?" he asked, his voice full of concern.

"No, but she's certainly more suspicious now Manny practically busted down the door. How'd he even know I was in Grady's office?"

"I don't know, but remember who Manny really works for?"

I let out a low whistle. "The Magician."

"Yeah. And George is suspicious, too. He caught Zalo foraging at our place."

I groaned. "We need to think this through. Meet me at Newspaper Rock?"

"Be there in twenty."

Seventeen minutes later, I slammed on Tilley's brakes at the dirt road entrance to the ranch. Standing outside the gate, Josh waved a hand through the swirling dust. "Want to open it?" I called through the window.

"Can't. It's locked." His boots crunched across the gravel, and he got in the passenger seat.

"You told me the last time we were here that it's never locked."

"I know." He scratched his jaw. "And someone posted new keep out signs along the fence."

I brushed my hair back from my eyes. "Josh, I'm worried. We need to talk to George."

97

Josh stared out at the desert for a moment. I waited. He needed time to consider all the angles. Finally, he nodded and climbed in the jeep.

I revved Tilley, threw her in gear, and we headed for the Trading Post.

****

George was locking up by the time we got back to Verde. With a big smile, he waved us inside the front door. He turned the old-fashioned deadbolt and headed toward the back of the store. "Hungry?"

Stupid question. Josh was always hungry. The guy'd grown another inch last month, and now towered over both George and me. Whenever I kissed him—Josh, I mean—I had to stand on tiptoe.

We walked through the store and pushed aside the curtain into their small kitchen. George crossed his arms and waited like he knew we needed something more than a tuna sandwich.

"George knows about Zalo," Josh said to me, and I nodded. No surprise he'd figure out his pantry was being raided every week.

It was my turn to spill it, and I heaved a breath. "Zalo isn't the only person we're hiding," I blurted. "My mother's staying with him in the Ruined City." It's always easier to get the worst part over with quickly. Well, almost the worst part.

George grunted. "Are they in trouble?"

"My mother is."

"Are you? Is Josh?"

Josh and I exchanged glances, and George grunted again. "How bad?"

I let the air rush out of my lungs. "My mother was convicted of murder, for killing my father." I held up my hands to ward off George's exclamation. "She didn't do it, honest, but she escaped from jail last month. The police and a really bad guy are hunting her. They may be hunting us now, too."

Josh frowned, shaking his head, but he added. "We think he and the Magician are old enemies."

George sucked air. "Real bad."

****

George chopped a couple of onions and started a batch of his famous chili. The room filled with its delicious aroma, and my mouth began to water.

Josh and I sat at the table, giving the old man time to think about all we told him.

Josh had filled him in on the scary reading he got off the campaign poster and the creep who called himself Laurence.

I explained about the interview with Grady that afternoon, and how Manny had jumped in to stop it. Josh was worried about who sent the information to the police. I think we both suspected it was our big, bad dude.

Who'd sent Manny rushing in like the cavalry? I suspected the Magician. Kinda creepy if Josh's ghost could watch us. I rubbed the goose bumps climbing up my arms. No. Really creepy.

I watched Josh twisting his shoelaces. I thought he should tell George about the ancient pot he found on the cliff during the flood. It was his call, but George needed the complete picture. We stared at each other across the kitchen table, and I shot Josh a questioning look.

The only noise was the sizzle of cooking meat and onions. It smelled delicious. Even as worried as I was, I was hungry too. I was about to get up and grate cheese

99

when someone knocked loudly at the door.

Josh opened it, and Grady stepped inside. She didn't say anything, just kept staring at the floor. Her mouth was pinched into a tight frown. Manny followed her into the room and closed the door. With his heavy brow drawn down over his dark eyes, anyone could tell he was worried.

"I'm afraid I owe you an apology, Forrest." Grady straightened her shoulders. "I'm sorry I scared you this afternoon." She glanced over at Manny, and I swear she blushed. My fingers literally itched to do a read on them.

Manny put his finger to his lips and signaled for us to follow him outside. He closed the door quietly before Grady cleared her throat and continued in a hushed tone. "I'd received an anonymous tip and was following up on it, but Sergeant Gutierrez has discovered something all of you need to know."

Everyone glanced at Manny, then back at Grady. "My office has been bugged," she said.

My heart did a little race around the dumpster, and I gulped loudly enough for everyone to hear. Not good news.

Manny crossed his arms and settled into a wide stance. "Someone other than the northern California police is hunting for a woman named Angela Morgan," he finally said. "They must be damned desperate to pull that idiotic stunt."

Even though Grady's announcement was a new glitch in the mystery, we could trust Manny to help us. Having him on our team was almost as good as having the Magician. Maybe better. Totally human and already working as a federal agent on the reservation, Manny also served as the Magician's new apprentice, and he was somehow wired into what the old ghost wanted.

Manny helped Josh and me more than once with the search for the burial raiders, and he saved our butts when Sheriff Robb kidnapped and was planning to kill us.

Grady continued. "The sergeant and I spent the rest of the afternoon researching why the authorities want this Angela Morgan, but so far her files are inaccessible. We know nothing about what she did or where she was being held. Not so much as a picture or a fingerprint is filed anywhere we could access."

Manny aimed a searing look directly at me, and my pulse again shot into the stratosphere. My cheeks must have turned bright red. I could feel the burn.

"It's time to let us help, Forrest," Manny said, almost gently. "You and Josh can't do this on your own."

I licked my lips and hesitated, but Josh took my hand and gave me a quick smile. "He's right."

"Angela's my mother," I said quickly before I could chicken out. "She was convicted of murdering my dad, but she's innocent. She was framed. My mom thinks Laurence Patterson, or whatever he called himself then, murdered my father."

"Can she prove it?" Grady asked.

George pointed his finger in the air and turned to Josh. "Wait a minute. Patterson? That's the man who ran in the Arizona election last year?"

Josh and I nodded.

"The guy spoke to us when Forrest was lost in the flood," George elaborated.

"Same guy," Josh said. "Who knows? He could

have been spying on us even then."

Grady moved closer and stared me down. I had to blink a few times to clear my vision.

"I'm listening."

I had to trust someone, so I blew out a long breath and began the sad story. "When I was little, Patterson worked with my parents in California. They were part of the ecology movement in northern California, working to save the old growth forest. My mother suspected Patterson of illegal activities and tried to stop him.

"Then Patterson murdered my father and framed my mother. My mother has been tracking him all these years from jail. Somehow he found out, and he's after her. She was in danger behind bars, so she escaped, but now we think he's after us, too. Josh and I are trying to figure out what the guy really wants."

"Does your mother know what he wants?" Manny asked.

"I don't think so. At least she hasn't told us yet. She's very secretive. She wanted me to take my grandmother and leave town. I wouldn't. We've been trying to convince her we can help."

Manny snorted at this last revelation.

I stuck my chin in the air. "Look. You have to admit, we caught Sheriff Robb with the evidence you needed to convict him."

He crossed his massive arms. "After he kidnapped you. What would have happened if I hadn't found you on that cliff when I did?"

"I admit, you helped, but we were the ones who set the trap."

"Yeah, a trap that almost got you killed."

****

A cold wind whipped down the alley, and I shivered in my lightweight sweater. "Why are we standing out here in the cold?" I finally had the nerve to ask.

Grady pulled on her short ponytail before she explained. "The sergeant believes your Trading Post might be bugged, too."

"I'll check it out now." Manny silently opened the door and disappeared inside. Several minutes later he returned and shook his head. "Nope." He pocketed a small black device that closely resembled a phone.

George blew a long, ripe raspberry, and we returned to the warmth of the kitchen.

Shoulder to shoulder, I sat next to Josh, chewing on my last fingernail. I'd relayed most of my story, but I held back on where Mom was hiding. It seemed traitorous, like I was snitching on her if I revealed her hideout in the canyon.

"Where is your mother, Forrest?"

I stared at the floor.

"I promise." Grady leaned closer and looked me straight in the eye. "We will keep your mother in protective custody until we can work out this mystery. No one will hurt her. No one but the people in this room will even know where she's being held."

My stomach clenched in painful knots, and I stared at my feet again. Josh and George were silent. This was my decision, my problem to solve. And it would be my fault if anything happened to my mom.

"She's in the canyon, near the Ruined City." I hoped mom would understand, but my stomach still swirled with worry. I felt like a traitor.

103

Manny nodded. "Good."

I gulped down the bad taste in my mouth.

Josh squeezed my hand and smiled.

Manny rose and turned to Grady. He grabbed the doorknob, preparing to leave. "Too dark now. We'll hike in first thing in morning."

I stood. "I'm going with you."

"No," Grady said. "Let us handle this."

"Grady, please. My mom needs to understand why I told you where she is. That it's best for everyone." I pushed back my chair and held out my palms. "Please give me time five minutes to explain."

Manny gave a nod. "Okay by me," he said, but Grady didn't seem convinced. She shook her head with authority.

I let the tears fall, and I could see by her face they did the trick.

We decided would leave at dawn, and, even better, Josh would come with us.

The next morning, when we rounded the final bend in the river, the campsite was empty. The fire pit was cold, scattered, like no one had stayed here for centuries. The Ruined City was deserted.

****

George paced back and forth in front of the potbelly stove. The weather had turned cold a couple of days ago. I'd started a fire early that morning, and the comfortable smell of wood smoke hung in the room. I pulled my hoodie over my ears and held my hands close to the stove to warm them. The holiday meant no school, no track practice, but we had a new problem.

Camp Verde buzzed with speculation. No one knew who'd purchased the ranchland which included

Newspaper Rock. George told me the sale was handled by lawyers in New York, and the previous owners had moved out quickly without even saying goodbye to their neighbors.

Rumors of lost gold mines and fracking operations rippled through our small reservation and the town. The tribe appointed George to approach the new owner about access to the sacred site, but the owner, hidden behind a dozen holding companies, had yet to arrive and claim the land.

After George spent days on the phone with the tribal lawyers, we were no closer to the answers we needed. I had my suspicions, but kept them to myself.

I rubbed my cold hands together. "I need to tell you one more thing." I tried to sound cool. Like the Magician's ancient water pot was no big deal, right?

George turned and stared at me. "I'm waiting."

I rubbed my hands on the front of my jeans. This wasn't going to be easy. "The Magician left me another artifact."

George stood quietly while I told him about the flood and how I found the rattler's den underneath the rock.

He drew his hand down his face and made a clicking sound with his teeth and lips. "I figured the Magician was mixed up in this somehow. What did he give you?"

"I'm not exactly sure. It's a ceramic pot, not very big." I held up my hands to demonstrate. "Not too pretty, either, but I think it's very, very old."

"What did he tell you about it?"

"Nothing. That's the problem," I shrugged. "I finally did a reading on the pot the other day, but the

Magician interrupted it. Someone…something evil was part of the vision."

"The Magician didn't want you to see who this person is yet?"

"Maybe. I did see a sacrifice."

"A blood sacrifice?"

"A child." I couldn't help a small shiver, and scooted my chair closer to the stove. "Zalo thinks the pot might be from Central America, part of an earlier culture, Toltec or Mayan. Maybe the Magician owned it later."

George sat down on the rocker, and the old wood creaked with his weight. "How does Zalo know?"

"He claims he's a Keeper of Stories, like his grandmother."

"Yes. I've heard of her. She's been dead several years. Many of the Hopi were afraid of her power, and some even thought she was a witch. It's probably why no one would take the poor kid in after she died."

"I'm worried about Zalo." I stood and paced the room, too revved up to sit still. "He disappeared along with Forrest's mom. He hasn't left a message, hasn't contacted us. Forrest is frantic. She wants to go search for him, but we don't even know where to start."

"Humpf," George said.

I had to agree. What a humongous mess.

"Zalo will return," George said mysteriously. "And so will Angela."

I stopped and stared at him. "What do you know?"

George sat in his old rocker with a grunt. "All in good time, Josh. All in good time."

****

Saturday morning I took the bus up the hill and met

106

Forrest in Jerome. She'd finished work at the Connor Hotel early, and George didn't need me to help at the Trading Post.

Forrest's grandmother had a client at her store, so we needed to bug out, but we didn't have track practice until two.

I took Forrest's hand as we crossed the busy road crammed with tourists, and climbed the steep steps to the little park above. At least here we had a place to ourselves.

Forrest sat on the old board swing, pushed her feet back and then forward, soon moving in a wide arc. For a few moments she was silent. Her eyes were closed in concentration, or maybe joy. Sometimes it was hard to tell with her.

I didn't feel like having my stomach heave and seize up, so I sat on the other swing, my arms folded around the chains.

"I still haven't heard from my mom, Josh. It's been more than a week. No call. No letter," Forrest finally said. "I'm scared."

I rubbed my jaw and nodded. "Zalo either."

Where had they gone? Were they in trouble? Had they left the Ruined City together, or gone in separate directions? When would they return?

I told Forrest about George's mysterious proclamation.

Forrest looked ready to cry. Her face turned pink, and her mouth crumpled.

I stood, grabbed the swing and pulled her close, kissing the top of her head. She let out a long sigh and relaxed into me. With one hand, I stroked her hair, soft and warm from the fall sunshine.

She drew back and studied my face. Her waterfall eyes were brimming with tears. "I'd finally found her. Finally gotten her back."

"I know." I brushed my thumb across her wet cheek.

She smiled through her tears and reached up to give me a salty kiss. "I can't lose her now."

"Stop."

Her eyes opened wide. She looked surprised, then confused. Her brows lowered, and she started to pull away. "S-sorry," she whispered.

"Just listen, Forrest. Stop tearing yourself apart."

She started to cry. In between sobs, she choked out, "I told on her. That's why...that's why she ran. She t-trusted me, and I let her d-down."

I leaned over, and nose to nose, caught her gaze again. "I think she was gone even before you spoke with Grady."

"Seriously?"

"Yes, seriously. Look. Your mom's a savvy lady. She needed to go somewhere. Do something or learn something. Maybe something important. She loves you, Forrest, and she will come back. I know it."

Forrest brushed away her tears and nodded several times, like she was trying to believe what I said. "You're right. She's strong. And smart. I shouldn't be so...freaked out."

"She will come back," I repeated slowly.

"Yes."

This time I think she almost believed me. I squeezed her shoulders gently. "We still have to do what we can to figure out this mess."

She sniffled and gulped down her tears. "How?"

I rocked her in my arms for a moment. "I don't know, but I'm working on it."

"Okay. Let's work together." She sat down and started to swing again, kicking her feet out and flying with a determined expression on her face. Then she turned to me, and a smile flashed across her face. "Remember what you said about fishing? That you have to know what the fish wants in order to catch it?"

I nodded. "Remember the bug in Grady's office? Patterson knows who you are and who you're related to. We can't send you to spy on him now."

"True, but I still know a way to catch our fish." Smiling fully for the first time today, she leaned far back in the swing, allowing her legs to stretch forward and pushing her toes toward the deep blue sky.

"Tell me what you're planning."

"Mom said Patterson wanted land when they were in northern California. Presumably she thinks he's buying up land in this area, too."

I still wasn't sure where she was headed.

"Don't you see? What other land has been sold recently right here in the valley?"

"The ranch?"

"And why would someone buy a scruffy old ranch that couldn't feed a half-dozen goats in a good year?"

I stood up quickly. "Based on what's been going on, I bet Patterson knows the land has sacred meaning."

"Bingo." But she skidded to a stop.

The dust rose around her. I grabbed her and kissed her. "So you think Patterson's buying up sacred land?"

She took hold of my hands. "Maybe he already owns other spiritual land."

"Okay, but why?"

She shrugged, but she was still smiling. "The Magician needs to explain. I have a feeling it has something to do with vortexes."

CHAPTER 10

"It's bait, George." I shoved my hair back in frustration. All three of us were crowded into his small office at the back of the closed store.

George's scowl deepened, and harsh lamplight highlighted the worry lines on his face. He double-checked the bug detector Manny'd left behind. "It'll never work."

"It will," argued Forrest. "Don't you see? Somehow our suspect bought Newspaper Rock. The place means something to him."

"It means everything to the Yavapai tribe," George ground out. "Newspaper Rock is a holy site. A *sipapu*, a place for the spirits to enter and leave this world."

"So this is how we get the land back." Forrest laid her palms flat on the desk. "By tricking this super-creep. We'll push Patterson until he shows us what he's really after and why."

"I sure as hell can't sell off a chunk of the Yavapai reservation, even if I wanted to," George argued. "The land belongs to the whole tribe. It's in a treaty, signed by the federal government. Patterson would never believe it."

Forrest shot a nervous glance my way. "Maybe George is right. Patterson's smart. Devious. Look what he did to my parents. He got away with murder."

I paced the small room. Were we crazy to go up against someone so powerful? So evil?

She stopped moving and stared at me, as if a great idea had just popped into her head. "Could you ask the Magician?"

Ah, but where was my damn ghost now I really needed him? I clenched my fists. "It's been weeks since I've seen him. And I've been to the cat petroglyph and the salt mine." I gave a quick, helpless shrug. "No spook."

I turned back to my cousin. "You're the only one who can do this. Patterson knows us. He's seen me in the visions, and heard Forrest in Grady's office. He would suspect us if we approach him."

"What if we ask Manny to help? Maybe Grady, too?" Forrest offered. "They could protect us."

George twisted his mouth back and forth like an old cow thinking about green grass.

We waited.

"Maybe." he finally said.

Forrest took hold of my hand and gave an excited, jump-up-and-down squeal.

George pointed a finger at both of us, waving it under our noses like we were three years old. "We need to take this slowly. Carefully. Dangle the bait and draw our fish to the surface."

"Agreed," we said in unison.

George still scowled. "He's one slippery dude."

****

I growled at the computer, pushed back my chair, and went to get a cold drink from the case at the front of the store. I popped the can and took a long draw. Today had been warmer, and the store felt stuffy.

George glanced up from reading the paper by the unlit stove with a quizzical look. "Problem?"

"I'll figure it out. I can't get the accounts to add up."

George grunted and went back to his reading. "If you're off a few cents, Josh, I told you, I don't care."

I started back toward the small office we used for files and billing. "It's more than a few cents."

I scratched my chin and frowned at the computer screen. I'd run the numbers twice, and each time the total came out wrong. Had I entered a number in the wrong column of the spreadsheet? I double-checked every one of the figures. No. There was no reason to be off exactly five hundred dollars.

A couple of minutes later, George poked his head in through the office door. "Uh, Josh. Look. Don't worry about the bills right now. It's not the end of the month yet. You still have a few days, almost a week. Why don't you go hang with Forrest?"

"She's working a long shift at the hotel today. High season." I squinted at the monitor. Where was that damn money?

"How about one of the guys on your team?"

I shook my head. "Midterms next week. Coach said we have to mega-study all weekend."

"Then go study."

"I'm ready for my tests. Already aced my chem test last week." When I glanced up at my cousin, the truth plowed into me. I narrowed my gaze.

George was acting super nervous. With his hands dug in his jean pockets, he'd licked his lips twice since he walked into the office. He moved from foot to foot as he spoke. He wouldn't look me in the eye either, even when I tipped my head forward and tried to catch his direct attention. Tells.

When I leaned back, the old wooden chair squeaked, and I crossed my arms to study him more closely. As I stared at him, he hitched his pants and pulled on each of his long braids, first one and then the other. Definite tells.

Something was up. Forrest had filled me in about how cops use tells to interview a suspect to determine if they were hearing the truth. Damn. My cousin was lying.

"What'd you do with the money?" I asked with no inflection in my voice.

He squared his shoulders and did his best to look annoyed. "Whaddya mean?" Then his eyes shifted first to the left and then to the right. Another tell.

"I mean we have exactly five hundred dollars missing from our business account, and in all the time I've done the books, we've never been off more than forty-three cents."

He scratched his nose, like he was thinking. "Maybe the computer's broken."

There. His gaze shifted left again.

I sucked in a quick breath and opened my eyes in surprise. He was *so totally* lying.

It didn't make sense. George was the most honest man I'd ever known. Disgustingly honest. He even gave change back at the grocery store if someone handed him too much. And he'd never let me lie about my age to sneak into the movies for cheap.

I frowned and stared at him silently, like he always did with me when I'd filched some candy from the jar by the cash register.

George glanced at my you-are-so-busted expression, and his shoulders dropped. "Aw, hell. I hoped you wouldn't notice."

"You hoped I wouldn't notice five hundred dollars? Where is it?"

"Made a loan to someone." He sat down in the other office chair and rubbed his hand across his mouth, and then glanced at the bug detector. He leaned toward me. "She promised she'd pay me back before you did the accounts at the end of the month."

"She?"

"Angela," he mouthed the name.

"Forrest's mom, Angela?" I had dropped my voice too, although the bug detector still hadn't found even a moth in our store.

George shrugged and threw out his hands, palms up.

I must have dropped my chin a foot or two. I know I stared at him for more than a minute while I gathered my thoughts. "What...?"

"Bus fare...food..."

"Where'd she go?"

"They." George confessed in a whisper. "Angela took Zalo to Mexico."

I threw my head back, closed my eyes, and let out a long, frustrated groan. "Why didn't you tell us? Forrest has been frantic about her mom."

"They needed time to get away. Angela was afraid if you or Forrest knew, Grady might be able to drag the story out of you."

"We'd never..."

"I know, but Angela didn't want you to have to lie. By keeping you out of the loop, you've remained above suspicion."

"Okay, okay. I get it." I shook my head in disgust. "But how will Angela get across the border? She's a fugitive. The cops'll be watching for her and arrest her. Plus, Zalo's too young to travel in Mexico on his own."

"Angela wouldn't tell me, but she insisted she had a way. She knew someone, a friend who would help her." George stood and put his hand on my shoulder. "I'm sorry, Josh. I hated keeping secrets, hated upsetting Forrest, but I couldn't think of any other way. We had to keep everyone safe."

"I understand." I gave him a big smile. "I have to tell you, George, you suck at lying."

"I think," George laughed aloud, "that's a good thing."

"When will they be back? It's been more than a week since we hiked out to the Ruined City."

George hissed in air between his teeth and looked worried again. "I expected them three days ago."

****

Honest. I wasn't freaked when Josh told me about my mother's scheme. Well, not too freaked. He was right about one thing. Mom was a savvy lady, with a gift that could keep her out of trouble. Hopefully.

But why Mexico? Had they gone so Zalo could learn more stories from the shamans? Or to keep my mother beyond the reach of the feds? It was so totally frustrating to sit here and wait. My cuticles were bleeding.

On top of that, Josh was furious with his ghost. There'd been no sign of the Magician for weeks. No spooky appearances. No visions to interpret. Apparently we'd have to deal with the living on this case without the help of the dead.

So George dug in his safe and found the deed to a worthless, out-in-the-boonies chunk of desert land he inherited from his uncle years ago. Josh and I hiked out to the site and salted the area with a few artifacts reaped from George's stock at the Trading Post, just in case someone tracked down the property.

None of the pieces were worth much, but they looked pretty authentic when we half buried them in the dirt. The real topper was the old skull Josh bought from a retired science teacher online. Totally spooky.

Then we started the rumors. That part was fun. Before long, everyone in town was whispering about a new discovery. A grave in the desert, found by accident. Was there treasure?

The big city newspapers even picked up on it, since Josh was already famous for finding the cat necklace. Of course it didn't take long for the media to hype a few old broken pots into the lost wealth of the Incas.

George practiced his lying before he went the Tribal Council and reported the artifacts were indeed valuable. They needed to be relocated for preservation, and the task would take months. He claimed ownership of the land, and insisted that because it was an ancient burial site, he had rules to follow, traditions to respect, and mounds and mounds of federal red tape to dig through.

We kept the location a hush-hush secret, but he hinted to the council that he'd placed guards on the site to protect the relics.

We'd baited the hook. Now we had to wait for our fish to strike.

****

116

I was stocking shelves after track practice Thursday evening when the first lawyer sleazed in through the door. Tall but paunchy, he had thinning hair and mean eyes. He glanced around the store with a smug expression and asked for George.

"Sure," I wandered slowly into the office and jerked my head toward the front. "Here fishy, fishy, fishy," I whispered.

George drummed his hands on the desk and grinned. "That didn't take long." He moseyed up to the counter at the front of the store. "I'm George Kwail. May I help you with something, sir?"

I hid out in the office, but could still hear everything on the monitor. We'd installed a surveillance system years ago. Even a trading post has the occasional desperate shoplifter.

"I have an offer for you, Mr. Kwail," said the Suit. He adjusted his red power tie and glanced around the shop with a sneer.

I held back a chuckle. No way the guy was from around here. His dark three-piece suit and short, clipped-and-gelled hair shouted New York or LA.

George nodded to the visitor and morphed into his wise-old-Native-shaman disguise. I covered my mouth to hold in the laugh. He crossed his arms like some Hollywood actor, hooded his dark eyes, and frowned at the guy. George could put on a pretty good act when he wanted to. I almost laughed again as the two stereotypes stared each other down across the counter.

"I'm waiting," George finally said.

The lawyer produced an envelope from his inside pocket and slid it across the glass. Without another word, he turned and walked out of the store, fancy shoes clicking on the wooden floor.

After the door closed, I joined George by the counter. Silently, the two of us stared at the letter. Even as my stomach did a couple of flips, I reached to pick up the envelope.

"Don't touch it."

From the junk drawer under the glass counter, George dug out a pair of white gloves he used for handling real artifacts. I shifted from foot to foot while he crammed his big hands into them.

The envelope wasn't sealed, just tucked closed. He opened it carefully, stared at the page inside, and then blew out a disgusted sigh.

"What's it say?" I peered over his shoulder.

He smoothed the paper onto the counter.

Written in plain block letters…"NICE TRY."

"Damn," we both said at exactly the same time.

"Want me to take a read on it?" I asked.

"He didn't touch this," George growled.

I placed my hand on the paper. George was right. Nada.

He folded the paper back into the envelope. Eyes narrowed, mouth tight, he stomped toward the front of the store and locked the door, but more than anger showed in the rigid set of his shoulders. My gut clenched. George was scared.

"What do we do?" I asked, getting more and more nervous myself. I swallowed hard and felt my Adam's apple bob in my throat.

George rubbed the side of his nose and pinched his hand over his mouth. "Got me." He wandered over to his chair by the stove and sat down heavily.

I let him rock for a while. Finally he glanced

toward me.

"Better call Forrest," he said in a quiet, determined way.

I nodded and pulled my phone from my pocket. "What…?"

"Tell her to be careful. This guy's on to us, and he's one very smart fish."

****

Several hours later, George and I headed for a meeting at the canyon. Seemed like the desert was the only place we could talk without feeling like someone was spying on us. I stopped by Grady's office, too, and she said she'd find Manny. Forrest wouldn't be thrilled, but we needed their help.

When we arrived, the two cops were already sitting on a high, flat rock, staring out at the canyon below. A cold storm off the Pacific threatened rain, and the sky shifted quickly between racing gray clouds and flashes of blinding sunlight. Avoiding the river, we gathered on the cliff above.

A couple of minutes later, Forrest drove up in Tilley again. The pink paint job glowed in the dawn light like a bottle of Pepto. She hurried over, and one brow lifted when she noticed the cops, but she didn't comment on their presence.

"Sorry I'm late," she said, a little breathless. She held up a small envelope. "I have news."

I folded an arm around her shoulders to give her a quick squeeze. She was trembling with excitement. Her face was flushed and her breath quick.

She flashed me a grin. "It's from Mom. She and Zalo will be back tomorrow."

Grady frowned, the lines on her forehead drawing

down into the V-shape of an arroyo. "She's a fugitive, Forrest, a convicted murder." She held up her palm to ward off Forrest's quick defense of Angela. "I know, I know, but I can't let her wander around free. If I see her, I'll have to arrest her."

Manny growled something about being a stickler, but nodded his agreement and turned to Forrest. "Keep her out of sight."

CHAPTER 11

I watched for Mom all the next day, expecting her to show up in some crazy disguise, but she didn't arrive until the next night. She must have been watching Gran's store, Angel's Cloud, from someplace nearby.

A few minutes after Gran left the store to meet a client for a Tarot reading, I heard a knock on the back door. I opened it, gave a shout and rushed into my mom's arms.

She laughed and hugged me tightly, but then stood back and put a finger to her lips. She pulled me out onto the narrow porch behind the store and closed the door. I hugged her again, and I felt wonderful, all warm and fuzzy, even though everything was a total disaster.

Zalo waited silently behind her, and gave me a quick wave when I noticed him. They both looked exhausted but excited.

"We've been so worried," I said.

Mom smiled and brushed her warm hand across my cheek. "We're fine."

"Should I call Josh?"

"Not yet." She glanced overhead. "Could you turn off the porch light?"

I reached inside the door to flip the switch. In the dim light glowing from our upstairs kitchen window, I could still make out her expression. I sensed her nervousness, and an uncomfortable tingle scooted up my spine.

121

She folded her hands around mine and stared at me with an expression I'd never seen before. Goosebumps rose and rippled over my arms. I shivered. Fear? I swallowed hard. Mom looked totally freaked out.

Then she squared her shoulders and firmed her mouth, as if to summon her courage. I searched for mine, but shivered again.

"You need to be very careful, Forrest," she whispered.

"You too." I repeated Manny's warning to stay out of sight. "I'm sorry, Mom. We were so worried. We needed their help."

"It's okay. You didn't have a choice by then."

I glanced back and forth between Zalo and my mother. "What'd you learn?"

"Later," she replied and slipped a note into my hand. "We'll be here. It's a derelict cabin out in the mountains east of Verde. Bring Josh tomorrow. No one else. And Forrest, make sure you aren't followed."

"Can't you stay, just for a little while? Gran won't be—"

"The store's bugged," Zalo whispered. "HE'D hear us."

"Bugged?" I swallowed once, then again, but bile rose and burned in the back of my throat. "How do you know?"

"We followed one of Patterson's guys, and your mom read his mind from across the street." Zalo shot me a brief smile. "Pretty cool, huh?"

"But Manny checked out the shop one day when Gran was out. He said we were safe."

"Things change, but you are safe, darling, for now. Patterson is paranoid, but doesn't believe you're a real threat to his plan." She rubbed my arms to comfort me. "Just be careful and don't give away that you know about the devices."

Zalo tugged at Mom's elbow and headed down the steps.

"We should leave now." She gave me another hug, and I returned the gesture with all the love I could give her. When she pulled away, my eyes overflowed with tears. Hers did, too.

"Don't let Patterson know," she repeated, and they disappeared into the darkness of the narrow alley.

I rubbed my palms up and down my arms to ward off the damp, wintery air. I stared at the knob on the back door. I was freezing out here, but I dreaded going back inside. Were there listening devices upstairs, too? In our kitchen? In my bedroom?

Stupid. Why hadn't I demanded Manny leave a detector with me?

I paced the narrow landing, trembling with cold and anger. No, terror. How long had the creep been spying on us? At least a week. I ground my teeth until my jaw cracked, grabbed the cold, metal stair railing and growled into the night. I should toss the place, find the devices and grind them up in the garbage disposal.

"No," I whispered to the frigid wind. "Then you'd know, you creep, and we can't let you win."

Leaning against the wall, I fisted my hands and stared at the lopsided moon in the eastern sky. I had to calm down, big time. I breathed in the frosty air through my nose several times before I could steel myself enough to open the door, but I grabbed an unused trash can and walked into the house, so it would look like I'd just come back from taking out the garbage.

I dead-bolted the locks on the doors and started up the stairs. Patterson and his cronies could hear me, but could they see me, too? Even in the warmth of our upstairs living room, another chill rippled down my back.

I clicked on the TV and upped the volume. Canned laughter blaring from a sitcom was better than the heavy silence of our tiny living room. I curled up on the couch with a gaudy throw Gran crocheted and tried to stop shaking. No way was I going to bed when that perv could be watching.

I'd talk to Josh tomorrow. In person. For all we knew, our phones were bugged, too. If Patterson could get away with murdering my father, he could get away with anything.

****

Forrest looked spooked when I saw her after third period. Her eyes were dull and bruised underneath, and she was still wearing the yellow shirt she had on yesterday. "I waited in the parking lot before school," I called as we met in the hall outside English.

"Bad night. Gran let me sleep in."

"What's up?"

She drew me out of the crowd of kids slamming lockers and hurrying to class. "Mom's back. Zalo, too," she said quietly in my ear.

"Great."

"She's freaked." She leaned very close. "Me too. The store's been bugged now. Maybe even being watched."

My mouth went dry, and I took a step back in surprise. "Should we tell Manny? Grady?"

"No," she almost shouted and several kids turned

to stare. She sucked in a raspy breath and shook her head as a sunset-colored blush flashed over her pale cheeks.

I pulled her into an alcove underneath the stairs. She was shaking like a twig in a sandstorm, and my gut plummeted. To hell with the PDA rules. I wrapped my arms around her, and she clung to me. The bell rang for fourth period, but we both ignored it. The last locker slammed, and the hall went silent. Finally, she stopped trembling.

"Better?"

She nodded into my shoulder.

"Now tell me." I managed a calm tone, even though my heart pounded like the bass drum in our school marching band.

She glanced up and down the hall. We were totally alone, but she still looked frightened. "Let's get out of here."

I gave her a quick nod, took her hand, and we ran down the back hall behind the gym. Skipping class was the least of our troubles. If we were busted and got detention, at least we'd serve the time together.

I glanced around the parking lot, looking for Tilley, but her pink jeep wasn't there. Forrest pointed in her Gran's old V-dub, jumped in, and started it up. I rode shotgun.

Forrest held on to the steering wheel with white-knuckled determination. She drove under the speed limit for a change, and even used her turn signal when she changed lanes. Who was this girl...I mean, woman?

She didn't say a word until we were a several miles down the highway, heading south out of Verde. When a couple of long-haul trucks whizzed by us, the little car shook.

Every few minutes her gaze veered toward the rearview mirrors. I rotated in my seat and checked out the road behind us. "You think we might be followed?"

Her lips thinned, and she gave a quick nod, but her eyes never left the highway.

"That's why you didn't drive Tilley."

"She's a little obvious."

"A little."

The corners of her mouth tweaked up in an almost smile. Then, without warning, she cut across three lanes and dodged off the highway at the next exit. Now there's the Forrest I love.

We waited underneath the bridge overpass. After holding our breath a couple of very long minutes, we knew no one had followed. Forrest leaned her head back against the seat rest and rubbed her shoulders.

"You okay?" I asked.

"Think so. Give me your phone."

I dug in my jeans and held it out.

"Better if you call George," she said, more to herself than to me. "Tell him we're going to be gone several days. Tell him not to worry, but to go see my gran and take her to lunch at the Haunted Hamburger before he gives her the message that I will be with you."

I shrugged and tapped in my cousin's number, but Forrest sat up quickly. "Wait. Tell him in Yavapai."

I switched languages and left the message. As I was about to stash the phone back in my pocket, she grabbed it and tossed it out of the car. "I know, I know," she answered my surprised look. "I'm paranoid, but 'he' could track us."

I gave her a quick nod. "Not worth taking a chance. I need a new one anyway."

We merged back onto the highway heading north toward the casino, and I kept watch out the back window. "I think we're clear. No one pulled a U-ey to follow us. Where are we going?"

Forrest swallowed hard a couple of times and handed me a scrap of paper. "See if you can figure out this map."

I studied the rough drawing and recognized Zalo's messy writing. "I know where this is."

"Good."

"Don't know if the Dub will get us too far. Pretty rough track."

"Then we'll walk."

****

And we did. Ten miles into the desert, the washboard road grew ruts the size of swimming pools and boulders the size of trucks. After we got stuck the second time, we gave up and parked the old car on the side of the road behind some tall mesquite trees.

Forrest dug in the front boot of the old car and handed me a jacket. She tugged on hers and pulled out a pack crammed with supplies. She'd put some thought into this plan.

"Yeah, I did. I had all night."

I glanced up in surprise.

"Sorry. I'm so hyped, I read you without thinking."

"No prob."

"Shouldn't we have called Manny? Grady?"

She shook her head fiercely.

"Forrest, listen. Sometimes it's okay to ask for help."

She was breathing quickly again, in scared little puffs, which billowed in the cold morning air. Her eyes narrowed. "No. Not yet. I need to see my mom. Find out what she knows."

I pushed back my hair in frustration. "This is crazy."

"Then I'll go alone." Her shoulders folded in on themselves, but she turned and hurried down the rough path like she knew where she was going.

Damn. She didn't. She'd be lost in five minutes, and it would be dark in an hour. The winter light was already starting to fade.

"Okay, okay." Swinging my pack up onto my back, I folded the map and shoved it in my pocket. "It's only a couple more miles. Let's go."

She turned and shot me a relieved smile. I gave her a quick kiss. "But we'll talk to them later if there's a problem. Right?"

"Maybe."

I took her cold hand in mine, and we hurried down the road together. I was still worried, but no way was I letting her out of my sight.

We'd have gotten there sooner if we'd brought our running shoes. It was almost dark by the time we hiked out to the location marked on the map. The weather was getting colder, and our breath steamed ahead of us as we climbed the last hill.

Low clouds, heavy with winter rain, hung over the desert, and the wind brushed fine drizzle through the air in long waves. The mountains were pale blue ghosts behind the thick mist.

Forrest filled me in on the meeting with her mom the night before. She was still freaked, but being closer to solving the mystery had me amped. If Zalo had answers, we had a chance to get ahead of Patterson.

I smelled wood smoke and knew the cabin was nearby. We left the trail, and from the top of a ridge we could see the shack, camouflaged inside a stand of stunted pines and juniper.

"Nice hiding place." Anyone walking along the beat-to-shit path who didn't already know to look for it would miss the shack entirely. We hurried down the hill, dodging through the high desert scrub of saguaros and piñon pines.

We neared the cabin, if you could call it that. One side of the front porch hung sideways, and the roof tipped at a crazy angle. I gave a shout, and the door screeched as Zalo pried it open and waved us inside.

The room was tiny, but someone had swept the rough wood floor with a frayed broom in the corner, and a fire blazed in the river rock fireplace. Even though rags were stuffed into the broken windows, the icy wind still whistled through the cracks. But the roof looked solid from inside with just one old coffee can set out to catch drips in the corner.

A couple of bricks and boards were the only furniture, but the fire was warm, and it gave the funky place a homey, almost safe feel. Angela sat crossed-legged on the floor, stirring a pot set in glowing embers. Something smelled good, and my stomach growled. A pile of empty soup cans sat nearby, with a dozen more stored in the corner along with a mega pile of cut wood.

"Found the cabin last spring when the canyon was flooding," Zalo answered before I could ask. "I put in a few supplies, thinking I might need the place again someday."

Forrest sat next to her mom. When Angela hugged her and kissed her on the cheek, Forrest leaned her head on her mother's shoulder.

I turned away to give them privacy to reunite. A sudden hollow moment of loneliness rushed over me, but I swallowed hard to push my feelings aside. Even though I would never have my mother back, I really was glad Forrest had hers.

CHAPTER 12

"Tell us about Mexico," Forrest said while Angela scooped dinner into Zalo's scavenged cups.

"There's time after dinner." Angela waved me over. "Here, Josh. All we have is foraged soup, but it's hot. Come have something to eat."

I sat on the floor next to Forrest and waited until everyone had their serving. Steam rose from the cups into the cold air of the cabin, and the warmth thawed my icy hands. We slurped it up without spoons, and canned soup had never tasted so good.

Forrest dug out power bars from her pack, and we ate those for dessert. She'd brought two for me, but I shared the extra one with Zalo.

After dinner, we sat in a close circle in front of the fire. Forrest's shoulders finally relaxed, and when I put my arm around her, she leaned into my side. She was breathing softly, and her mouth had softened into an almost smile.

I smiled, too. I glanced around the tiny room, with firelight winking off steamed-up windows. Funny how I felt more at home here than I had anywhere in a very long time.

I nodded my thanks when Angela poured me a cup of coffee. It was bitter, but hot. I blew on it and sipped carefully.

"Zalo," Angela said with an encouraging look, "tell

Josh what you learned in Mexico."

Forrest shifted closer to me. "Did you go, too?" she asked her mother.

Angela shook her head. "I took Zalo as far as the border near Nogales. I have a friend who took him into Mexico and traveled with him the rest of the way."

Zalo blew on his coffee and slurped. "It's not too tough for a coyote to take you INTO Mexico."

Forrest stared at her mom. "How do you know a coyote?"

Angela hesitated, and then opened her mouth as if to explain, but Forrest held up both hands. "Never mind. I don't want to know."

"Probably not," Angela said with a short chuckle.

Zalo settled his back against the fireplace. "The trip was a cinch, thanks to your cousin George. We had money for the bus, so we didn't have to hitchhike. I visited my aunt and uncle again, and they took me to meet a shaman from the highlands. He lives in the jungle, close to the southern border, near Guatemala. I spent several days with him and the other chiefs to learn what they knew about the Magician...and our friend Patterson."

Zalo stared straight at me, his bright, dark eyes lit with secrets. He was vibrating with excitement. "You know the origin story of the Hopi, but I'll tell give Forrest and Angela a quick version."

Straightening his shoulders, Zalo closed his eyes. He whispered under his breath for a few moments. His face calmed, and his eyes lost focus.

I had heard the legends many times from George, so I knew them by heart in both our ancient language and in Yavapai.

Although Zalo translated the stories into English he still flavored the tales with the cadence of our language. He had been granted the wisdom and poetry of his storyteller gift:

"He is called many names, but many of us believe in Tawa, the sun spirit." Zalo chanted in a soothing, singsong voice.

"He created the First World from Endless Space, and for a time the People lived in peace in the First World.

"But then there was fighting and dissension among the People. Spider Grandmother then led the good People to the next world through the sipapu."

"What's that?" Forrest whispered in my ear.

"It's a spiritual entrance, an opening to climb through," I whispered back. "There's one near Newspaper Rock."

Her forehead scrunched. "I've never seen a hole there."

Zalo opened his eyes. "It's not a *visible* hole." He sounded annoyed.

"Sorry," Forrest murmured. "Go on."

Zalo cleared his throat.

"So-o, over a great many years, the People traveled through the sipapu several times. Each of the worlds they lived in was different. The People and animals of each world changed.

"Many believe the Second World was destroyed by fire, and the Third World was destroyed by flood. But Spider Grandmother always saved the good People.

"After the flood in the Third World, Spider Grandmother led them into the Fourth. This is where

we live today. "

Zalo rested for a moment, his chin on his chest.

"Is there a fifth world?" Forrest asked me.

I nodded. "Skeleton Man guards the Fifth world. A person's spirit travels there when he dies. Our bodies remain in the Fourth, but our spirits move on through the sipapu."

She nodded in understanding. "Kinda like heaven."

Zalo smiled and took a noisy slurp of his no-longer-steaming coffee. He continued in the same quiet tone.

"When the People arrived in the Fourth World, they divided into groups, and each clan went on a long journey. Some traveled north, even as far as the Back Door, a place of cold and ice where other peoples had traveled from. Other clans traveled south to the narrow place between two oceans.

"Each group would stop and live for a while in a new place. They would build cities and farm the land, but then life would become too easy, and they would lose the balance that was necessary for a good life.

"And so the good People would move on. Finally the People arrived in our land, where we have remained for many centuries. Other clans have returned from their journeys and joined us. We have lived in balance and in peace, away from the rest of the world. "

Zalo stirred and opened his eyes. He turned to me. "Among the People," he continued in his quiet tone, "some have great knowledge and power. Shamans and Priests learn from the ancestors. They keep the People safe."

I straightened up, and my heart thumped a little

louder. I knew the responsibilities I would someday face as shaman of our tribe. Forrest and Angela stared at me, and my cheeks and ears warmed in the cold room.

Zalo's eyes opened wider. "The pot you showed me, Josh, is a very holy object. It was made many centuries ago in what we now think of as central Mexico, and was used in the religious traditions of that time.

"For sacrifices?" Forrest whispered.

"Yes. Many of the early cultures of Central America believed in blood sacrifice. Some sacrificed children. The Magician could have traveled from there and come north to this land."

Feeling light-headed with this news, I shifted my weight to regain my balance. "Maybe he traded for the pot and lived his whole life in this valley?"

"Possible, but I don't think so. I think he's much, much older than you thought. Patterson, too, although he served as apprentice to the Magician."

I rubbed my eyes hard and blinked several times to focus. Why had my spook kept these secrets from me?

"What about the necklace?" Forrest asked. "It's very different from the other items we saw in the Magician's grave."

Zalo rubbed his temples, like he needed to concentrate again. "Even before the Aztecs, the Toltec and Maya believed in shamans who could shapeshift into the Jaguar."

Forrest took my hand. "Do you think it's a clue? The Magician's necklace has the face of a cat."

My stomach swirled with her suggestion. "I've always assumed it was a symbol of his clan. Maybe it comes from an earlier time, but I've never seen..." I bit my lip to stop my words, but somehow Zalo caught my meaning anyway. His eyebrows rose in surprise. He studied me suspiciously. "Can you see the stories in these sacred objects?"

"Yes," I admitted.

Zalo turned to Forrest. "Can you?"

"Not with objects." Forrest glanced over at her mother. "I see the truth or the lies in people's words."

Zalo redirected his focus across the room. "I am very tired. I have more to tell, but I will wait for another time."

We moved back from our circle, and I stretched my tight shoulders. The fire had burned down to glowing embers, but the small cabin was still warm. We were safe for now. With darkness, even the smoke from the chimney was hidden.

Forrest could scarcely keep her eyes open. She leaned heavily against me.

Zalo yawned and curled up on the floor, using his coat as a blanket. Soon he was breathing slowly.

Angela added a log to the fire. "I can take the first watch. I'll wake you in a few hours. Then we need to talk."

I closed my eyes, but there was no way I would sleep.

I cuddled next to Forrest to keep us both warm, but my mind was too full of questions to sleep. Was the Magician really from this earlier time? Was he a participant in the Aztec sacrifice I'd seen in my vision? He'd never hurt me, but just who was he, and whose side was he on?

A hand shook my shoulder, and I woke with a start,

my heart pounding the way it did when I was reliving my usual bad dream. I looked around and recognized the small cabin where we'd taken shelter from the stormy night. Then I sat up, stretched, and rubbed my side until the blood returned to my arm and the numbness faded.

Outside the wind howled, and I wondered if the rickety shack would hold together one more night. The drips of water in the pan in the corner were constant, almost a steady stream, and heavy raindrops splattered against the makeshift windows. I shivered in the cold, damp room.

Angela tossed another log to the fire and sparks flew up the crooked chimney. This shelter was the only thing keeping us alive tonight. The freezing rain would have finished us off by morning. That is, if Patterson didn't find us first.

I covered Forrest with her coat. She moaned something and sank back into a deeper sleep. I touched her hair and tucked a curl behind her ear with a brief sigh. No matter how much danger we were in, she had her mother by her side. This was probably the first time she'd slept deeply in weeks.

I crawled closer to the fire and warmed my hands. Angela handed me some coffee, and I sipped. It tasted gross, but warmed my insides.

Angela smiled at the face I made.

"I'm awake. I can take this watch," I whispered.

Angela shook her head. "Let's talk first. Maybe after that I'll take a quick nap." She curled her knees up close to her chin and wrapped her arms around them. The flames licked at the new log and bounced more light into the room.

I leaned against the opposite side of the fireplace, and was about to speak when Zalo let out an enormous snore and turned restlessly in his sleep. He mumbled a few words and then settled down again.

Angela smiled to herself. "He does that a lot."

I had to laugh. "Not a great roommate?"

Chuckling under her breath, she shook her head. "No, but he's a very special boy." She frowned. "We need to find him a place to live, a safe place to grow up, not some ancient dwelling in the wilds of the desert."

"George and I have tried. He seems to like the canyon. He's…"

"Different?" she said, finishing my sentence.

All at once I could feel her reaching into my thoughts, and I slammed down my barriers to keep her outside my head.

She glanced away. "Sorry. I didn't mean to intrude."

"S'okay. We're all a little hyped. When she's wound up, Forrest reads me without even thinking."

I studied Angela's face in the firelight. "What do you want to tell me?"

She rose slowly, retrieved her backpack from the corner, and returned to the fire. "In the morning, I want you to take Zalo and Forrest and leave. Make a run for it. I would suggest taking George and my mother, too, but they will slow you down. Plus, they aren't in nearly as much danger as you three are face."

She unzipped a bottom pocket, and the wad of cash she pulled out took my breath away. Jeez. A huge stack of hundreds.

"Where…?"

"Don't worry. It's not marked or stolen. It's my

money, an inheritance from my father's family."

"Then why'd you borrow the five hundred from George?"

"I had this hidden away, and part of our trip to the border included retrieving this stash. Here, take it." She thrust the cash into my hands.

I opened my mouth to object, but she cut me off. "Listen, Josh. Patterson's very dangerous, and now he knows about all of you. Forrest, Zalo, and you. He wants to force me out of hiding, and he will not hesitate to hurt every one of you to accomplish that goal. Forrest's in the most danger because she's my daughter, but you all need to disappear. Now."

"She won't go," I argued. "I doubt if Zalo will either. They both love you."

"You have to make them."

"And how do I do that?" I said too loudly, and Forrest stirred in her sleep. I lowered my voice, but not my temper. "I couldn't even stop her from coming here. You have one helluva stubborn daughter."

"That old apple and tree thing?"

"Probably," I sighed and rubbed the back of my head on one of the smooth rocks of the fireplace. "But Angela, what the hell were you thinking? You should never have come back to Arizona."

"I tried to stay away." Angela glanced at Forrest and sucked in a trembling breath. "When I 'left' prison, I planned to head straight for Mexico, but I knew she was here, and the need to see her—just once more— was too powerful. I was only going to watch her from a distance, just check on her. Make sure she was happy."

"What changed your mind?"

"I was sitting in that little park in Jerome one

afternoon…you know, just enjoying the view and the quiet. Forrest ran up the stairs and went straight for the swings. I could tell she was upset, but she could see me, so I didn't say anything, just waited and watched. It must have been ten minutes before she worked off whatever was bothering her. I don't think she even knew I was there."

"She was on the swings, going as high as she could?"

"Yes. She wasn't crying. Just so…" Angela gazed at the ceiling "…angry. After about ten minutes, she dragged her feet in the dust and slowed the swing. She looked calmer and left, so I walked up the stairs toward town.

"That's when I saw an old priest sitting on the steps of the church, sunning himself. He smiled at me— patted the empty place next to him. I guess he saw how shaken I was." Angela swallowed hard and stared at her hands for a moment. They were gripped together so tightly, they'd gone gray from lack of blood.

She shook them briefly and continued, "Next thing I knew, I was telling him my whole damn story. Not about Patterson, but how I had just watched my daughter in the park, and she didn't even know me."

"He was a good listener. Let me rage a while, then cry. Then he patted my hand and said, 'You should go to her.'"

I stared at the fire to keep my cool.

Angela took my hand, hers icy in mine. I rubbed some warmth back into them.

"That was the day I came to see you, but now I don't know if it was the right thing to do."

I shrugged. "Everyone in town knows about that

priest, the troublemaker."

"Josh," she chided. "What a thing to say."

"Little old guy, thin gray hair, dusty hassock?"

"Yes. That's him. He was extremely kind."

"He's a ghost."

At first her eyes scrunched up, her mouth hanging open, but I guess she could tell I wasn't lying, because her face went pale. A sheen of sweat reflected off her cheeks and forehead in the firelight.

I instantly felt sorry for what I said. "Look. He's not a bad spirit. Mostly harmless. But your decision to involve Forrest in this disaster was a huge mistake."

Angela turned back to the fire. "I know, but at that point I had no idea how powerful Patterson had become." Pain and fear ripped across her face in terrible, crashing waves.

I swallowed hard and moved in close enough to feel her warmth. "So if Patterson's that powerful, why hasn't he killed you like he did your husband? He had to have known where you were the whole time you were in jail."

Her eyes darted around the room, and she bit down on her lip so hard I could see a hint of blood. She faced me again and shook her head. "I can't tell you."

My temper boiled higher again, and I gritted my teeth to keep my voice down. "Fuck it, Angela. You want my help? You can't keep secrets anymore. You have to tell the truth."

It took a moment, but she seemed to resolve the question in her mind. "You're right, of course."

I sat back, still breathing hard, while she brushed away the dampness under her reddened eyes. "Patterson learned of my gift when I knew him before, when we lived in California," Angela said. "Remember, at one point, I trusted him. Although he's brilliant and manipulative, reading minds isn't something he can do. He wants my 'talent.' Obviously I'm no use to him dead."

I grunted my agreement.

"I have fought him, resisted him, hidden from him, but he has grown so much stronger. I don't know why, but I suspect the power in the vortexes adds to his strength, or maybe his abilities to manipulate people. If he knew about Forrest's gift..." she shivered.

My stomach sank to the cold wooden floor. "He would grab her—use her."

"Yes, that's why I'm afraid. She isn't old enough, strong enough yet to resist him."

I gulped back the vile taste in my mouth and glanced over at the girl I loved. A powerful need to protect her surged through me and shook me to my bones. I hissed in a fearful breath.

"You are the only one," Angel whispered, "who can save her."

"What does Patterson want?"

"You mean besides world domination?"

I grimaced at her attempted joke. "I mean, all these years he has been working toward something. He wants something. Why the land grabs? What is it about the vortexes?"

Angela gave an enormous shrug. "I wish I knew, but I suspect your Magician can tell us."

I hung my head and sighed. "That's if my stupid ghost ever shows his face again."

I smelled coffee and opened my eyes, blinking against the first dim rays of golden light flowing in through the east-facing window. I yawned, stretched my stiff muscles, and sat up, rubbing my face

"He's kinda cute in the morning," Angela teased.

Forrest blushed. "I wouldn't know."

Her mom raised an eyebrow and then nodded. "Good."

After an early breakfast of canned peaches and stale crackers, Zalo stoked the fire and began his story again.

"The shaman from Guatemala told me many stories of the early times. I learned of their gods and the Hero twins. The legends of one culture were sometimes shared, sometimes changed by the next. The Olmec, Toltec, Maya, Aztec, and Inca all influenced our Hopi traditions.

"One powerful spirit seems to travel through all these times. He was called many names. He had many faces, but somehow there's always a connection."

My stomach tightened with excitement. "The Magician?"

Zalo shook his head. "No, I don't think so, but the Magician serves him. However, the Magician is more than a ghost."

"The Magician was a flesh and blood man when people lived in the Ruined City. He's shown me that time."

Zalo sat up straighter and focused on my face. "When you saw him, what did he wear? What did he do?"

My mouth went dry, and I licked my lips before I spoke. "He wore the necklace. He showed me the time when he etched the petroglyph of the saber-toothed cat."

"The Jaguar," Zalo said.

Forrest's hand shot out and squeezed my arm. "So the petroglyph and the necklace are important."

"The necklace was the Magician's first gift to me. Remember? After I returned the tools to his grave, he gave me the cat."

"And he was alive in the twelfth century?" Zalo repeated.

"Yes, I'm sure of it."

"He probably lived several earlier times, too," Zalo said. "The legends about him among the Toltec and Mayan people seem to fit. He was a good man, a wise leader, maybe a king. He's always associated with the Jaguar. A powerful Totem."

"Wow," Forrest whispered under her breath. We all nodded in amazed agreement like so many bobble-heads on a shelf.

"Do you have the pot with you?" Zalo asked me.

I nodded and reached for my pack.

Forest turned in surprise. "You do?"

"I could never decide where to hide it, so I made a spot in the top of my pack and carry it with me." I dug the tiny artifact out and pulled off the layers of bubble wrap.

Zalo took the pot in both hands and studied it almost reverently. "Yes. See the face here. See the way the mouth is turned into a fierce frown. This is similar to the Aztec rain god. It's a symbol for rebirth. Jaguar shamans are sometimes represented this way."

CHAPTER 13

"So who is Patterson? Or who was he?" Angela asked. "Is he the same age as the Magician?

"And why is he human when the Magician no longer is?" I added.

Zalo let out a sigh. His shoulders and chin drooped, and he stared at his hands. "Other powerful spirits exist. Some are evil. I think Patterson may be a manifestation of one of them. He and the Magician could be ancient enemies who have renewed their feud."

"Patterson was alive and up to no good more than fourteen years ago," Angela said. "I never tried to trace him further back than that, but maybe he's been around for much, much longer."

My foot jiggled with nerves, so I stood to walk off the feeling. "The Magician started haunting me about four years ago."

Forrest watched me pace the narrow room. "Who knows? Maybe he was spooking with someone else before you?"

"True," I agreed, "but didn't Manny say that was about the time the Magician recruited him?"

With an excited nod, Forrest turned to face her mother. "We need to find out what Patterson's been up to as far back as we can."

Angela twisted her fingers together and glanced over at me. I gave her a quick what-now? shrug.

Forrest glanced between the two of us. She

narrowed her eyes, and I felt her power dart through my thoughts. Her mouth dipped into an angry frown. "What's going on?

"Few secrets in this family," Zalo hissed under his breath.

I rolled my eyes. "Forrest, your mom wants the three of us—you, me and Zalo—to book it out of here."

"You mean the cabin?"

"The cabin, the town," I sighed in resignation, "probably the state."

"Now?"

"Now."

"No way." She turned to Angela. "Are you kidding? Leave you alone to deal with that horror?"

"I'm trying to pro…"

"Protect us? Like you protected us all these years? By leaving me and Gran alone?"

"That protection worked for years."

"Yeah, until you 'escaped' from jail. Now we have Patterson and the cops on our tail."

Angela wiped tears with the back of her hand and pleaded with me silently.

I tried again. "Forrest, listen. Your mom loves you. And Zalo, too. She wants to keep you both safe."

Forrest fisted her hands on her knees and drew in several deep breaths. Man, she was pissed. I could hear her grinding her teeth. Super pissed. But when she spoke, her voice was controlled.

Quiet.

Way too quiet.

"We are not going anywhere."

Angela crossed her arms. "For-rest."

"Don't you 'Forrest' me." She pointed an accusing

146

finger at her mother, and I moved out of the line of fire. "You came back. You let this cat, or jaguar, or whatever, out of the bag. I'm staying. I'm finishing this. Zalo and Josh…"

"I'm in too," Zalo said.

"Told you she was stubborn," I said to Angela.

Forrest huffed out a breath and stood. "I'll do the computer research. Trace Patterson as far back as I can."

Angela combed her fingers through her hair in frustration. "You don't have the codes I've…"

"Hacked?" Forrest finished the sentence.

Angela looked down at her hands.

"Give me what you can. I'll figure out the rest."

"What can we do?" Zalo asked.

"I think we need the necklace. I'll go get it," I said.

"I'll come with you," Forrest insisted.

"No. You need to get to a computer. If we drop you at the Trading Post, you can sneak in the back way and work in the office."

"On George's old dinosaur?"

"Best we can do," I said with a palm-up shrug. "You shouldn't go back to your place. No way it'd be safe for you at school or out in public."

Forrest chewed on her lip. "What about Gran?"

"She's okay for now." Angela rose and brushed off her jeans.

I stood too. "Okay. If we walk back to the car now, it'll be dark by the time we get into town. I can do my research at the Trading Post. You two drive up and get the necklace in Jerome, and then come back to pick me up. We can be back here by noon tomorrow, maybe sooner."

Angela reached for her coat. "I should go with you."

"No, Mom. The cops are bound to have an APB out on you by now. Having to keep you out of sight will just slow us down."

Zalo nodded. "You have to stay here."

Angela studied her daughter's face and then sighed. "I don't like this. If Patterson catches any of you, he can use you to take control."

"We'll be okay." Forrest gave her mom a hug and slung her pack over her shoulder. I'd already put on my coat and opened the door.

When we stepped outside, I checked the now overcast, leaden sky. "We're in for some snow."

"Snow? Here?" Forrest was incredulous.

"We're high enough."

Zalo sniffed the air. "We'd better hurry, dude. The weather's gonna get bad."

Angela pulled her jacket closer around her neck and waved from the droopy front porch, blinking back the tears.

Suddenly, my throat closed up tight. I leaned closer and whispered in Forrest's ear. "Go give your mom another hug before we leave."

****

"Hurry, Forrest," Josh called to me from the top of the rise. He and Zalo were moving fast over the frozen desert. I was lagging behind. My pack felt like a sack of rocks on my shoulders, and I stumbled over a rut. Josh grabbed and steadied me.

My breath steamed out as we ran down the rutted road together. My nose and cheeks and hands were frozen stiff. A few big, soft flakes of snow drifted down from the darkening sky.

The three of us finally made it back to the V-dub, but it was already dusk. Another twenty minutes, and we'd have been wandering around in the high desert in pitch-black night.

We climbed in and held our breath while the old car ground and wheezed a few times before it started, and then we headed for town. Since I'd never driven in snow, Josh took the wheel, concentrating on not getting us stuck in the washes and ice-covered potholes. I huddled in the passenger seat, worrying about our plan. And about my mother, all alone back there with a storm coming.

"Josh," I finally said after we had made it back to the gravel road and were going more than ten miles an hour, "I think we should stick together."

He glanced over at me. "How long will it take you to do your research on Patterson?"

I shrugged. "If mom's codes work, several hours."

"And if they don't?"

I blew out a quick steamy breath. "No way to know. Census info should be easy, but hacking into police databasis...."

"Then I'd better go get the necklace and come back for you. Otherwise we're wasting time."

Zalo leaned over from the tiny back seat. "Want me to ride up with you, dude?"

Josh shook his head. "No. Stay with Forrest in case something goes wrong."

I chewed on my nail. As much as I hated to admit it, Josh was right. It would take more than an hour for him to get up to the museum in Jerome. Add fifteen minutes to that, because he drove like a little old lady.

149

Plus more time to locate the curator who lived on-site, and con her into letting him have the necklace. Okay, more than a little time. Then an hour back down the hill, if he was lucky and it didn't snow anymore. Four hours, maybe five.

I could be halfway done with my research by then. If we finished up overnight, we really might be back out to the cabin by midday tomorrow.

He glanced over at me. "Got it all worked through?"

"Yeah. I just..." A sick feeling swirled in my stomach, and I swallowed hard to shove it down. Nothing to worry about, right? I was probably just hungry.

"I'll be fine." He took my hand and squeezed. "Nobody will recognize this old junker. Your gran hardly ever takes it out of the garage."

"Yeah, it's just..." The heavy feeling intensified, and I could almost reach out and grab the impression, but at that moment, we launched onto the main road. A streetlight glared into the car. I saw Josh smile, and my heart took a leap into my throat. The worry evaporated, and I smiled back at him. God, I loved the guy.

Josh grinned at me again. "I'll be back before morning."

"I guess it's the best we can do," I said, still wishing I was happier about the plan. It felt like my stomach and heart had somehow traded places.

Huddled to keep warm, the three of us crept down the main drag into Verde. Snow was falling more heavily by then, and the squeaky windshield wipers pushed lines of slush off the glass.

We passed one delivery truck parked on the

shoulder, and then the road was deserted. With our headlights turned off, Josh stopped the car at the back door of the Trading Post and yanked the brake.

It was dark inside. Even though it was just past ten, George was probably already in bed. Josh dug out his key and handed it over. "George sleeps lightly, so try to be quiet. If he wakes up, think of some story to keep him happy."

"He should know the truth," I argued as I opened the squeaky car door and stood in the slush-filled alley. Zalo flipped the front seat forward and climbed out stiffly. He ducked through the falling snow and stood, stomping his feet, by the door.

Josh leaned over the passenger seat to look up at me. "If George really pushes, tell him I'll explain everything when I get back tomorrow morning."

I started to say something, but then climbed back inside the car. I reached over the gear shift and planted my cold lips on his.

I wrapped my arms around his neck, and he kissed me back. We warmed up pretty quickly, and with a couple more deep kisses, my blood was pumping and I was wide awake. Our tongues touched and played together. Our breath came faster. I held on tighter. So did he.

"Be careful," I whispered in his so-soft ear and planted a row of little kisses down the warmth of his neck.

His hands roamed over me, lighting bonfires, even through my heavy clothes.

I sat back, panting. Now wasn't the time or the place. Too damn bad, but someday, somehow, we'd be together.

Josh still held onto my hands. "I love you, Forrest."

My eyes welled with hot tears, and one trickled down my face.

"Don't cry." He brushed the stupid dribbles from my cheek.

I kissed him once more, a big, salty kiss. "I love you too, Josh."

"See you in the morning," he said cheerfully as I climbed out of the car. Almost overwhelmed with dread, I put out my hand to stop him, but the V-dub's tires spun in the snow, grabbed, and he disappeared down the dark alley.

"He'll be okay," Zalo whispered.

I chewed on my lip and nodded. Silently, I slipped the key in the lock. We crept through the dark kitchen and back to the tiny office. The door squeaked when I closed it, but the Trading Post remained silent.

****

I felt bad lying to Forrest. Awful, in fact. I swallowed the bitter taste in my mouth and watched my friends disappear through the back door of the Trading Post. She'd be mega-pissed when she found out where I was really going. If she found out.

Even though I trusted Forrest with my life, the Magician had ordered me to hide his necklace from everyone. I had to keep my promise. No one—repeat, no one—knew where the treasure really was. Not even my cousin George was sure.

I raced out of Verde, hoping to outrun the storm, but the V-dub's wheels slipped wildly on a patch of black ice before they caught on fresh snow. Holding my breath, I hung on to the steering wheel and took my foot off the gas while the car slowed to a few miles an hour.

I held my impatience in check and crept forward into the howling night.

Hours passed before I was even close to my destination. The storm worsened, blowing waves of snow across the narrow road, and buffeting the little car. The snowflakes piled in the corners on the windshield, blocking my view. The little heater couldn't keep the fog cleared from the glass. I stopped again to wipe down the glass with my coat sleeve.

I squinted into the darkness and storm. Nothing but white. And cold. And wind.

I pulled my coat tighter around my ears and shivered. I'd never find my usual landmarks in this weather. With a curse, I slammed my fist against the dashboard.

No choice. I'd have to find shelter and wait until morning before I could go any further.

In the distance, a yellow light gleamed through the windblown snow. I let out an almost-happy shout. Finally I knew where I was, and my goal wasn't far. I crept down the road until I was under the pool of light, and parked. Safely sheltered at the gas station, I'd wait out the storm.

I must have drifted off for a moment, because I never heard the big car come up behind me. By the time I noticed it, huge lights glared through my back window, blinding me.

I waved. Maybe this guy had a better heater than mine? I grabbed for my door handle, but then his humongous black car smashed into my bumper and knocked me forward. The V-dub slid sideways across the icy pavement.

"Hey," I shouted in surprise, but by then the driver

had reconnected with my bumper. He revved his engine and pushed me onto the roadway.

I stomped on the brake, but my V-dub had no chance against the huge car.

For a second I was just pissed. Then scared. Then numb with terror.

My stomach turned over.

Then the whole car did.

Over and over, down the steep cliff, with the terrible sound of grating metal and the clatter and tinkle of breaking glass.

Black. White.

Black. White.

Pain.

I gasped for air, and more searing pain slashed through me. The cold wind blowing through the broken window froze my blood to my face.

I heard a car door slam and fought to open one eye. A flashlight beam traced over the snow. I could move one arm, and I realized I was upside down, trapped by the seat beat and the crushed roof of the car. I wanted to shout, but couldn't think clearly enough to make the sound. I sputtered and choked, my mouth full of blood.

Boots crunched over the icy snowpack, and a flash of silver toe points moved beside my head. I stilled with recognition, my heart pounding even harder.

Patterson.

The car rocked onto its side, and I cried out in agony, then struggled back from the edge of unconsciousness. Somehow I had to protect myself, or Patterson would kill me. He reached through the broken window aiming a gun at the side of my head. "Where are they?" he shouted, his face a mass of angry lines.

His power thundered around him.

"What?" I mouthed.

"Where are they? The necklace…the pot…"

I groaned against the unbelievable pain.

"I swear. I'll kill you now." He jammed the gun into my ear.

Something long and smooth stirred beside me and moved past my face. Huge rattles shook. An enormous snake slithered out the broken front window and into the snow.

Eerie purple light glowed over the landscape, and the howling wind silenced.

"No," Patterson shouted in frustration and fear. "You can't stop me forever."

Drumbeats sounded in the distance, growing louder, more intense.

"I will find a way," Patterson snarled, but he turned and disappeared into the night.

Pain engulfed me, tipping me over the verge into blackness. My last muzzy thought…*what is a rattler doing out here in the cold?*

****

George may tend to sleep lightly, but it was morning before I noticed him stirring in his room. I retied my ponytail, stood, and stretched out my stiff back. My mind and body were totally exhausted.

I heard a few unintelligible grumbles, some shuffling feet. A bedroom door opened. Soon I smelled fresh coffee, and my stomach growled at the thought of food.

I pushed back from the computer and poked Zalo. He'd passed out about four in the nearby chair. I ducked my head around the corner into the kitchen.

"George?" I whispered, hoping not to scare him.

He turned, surprised to see Zalo and me in the narrow hall.

"We'll explain in a sec. May I have a cup of that? It's been a long night."

"Where's Josh?" He poured each of us a steaming mug.

I took a quit sip of the hot coffee before explaining, "We have a lot to tell you. Do you want to get dressed first?"

George glanced down at his boxers and T-shirt, and blushed under his deep tan. Cussing softly, he hurried out of the kitchen and slammed the door to his room.

Zalo snickered, and we waited at the kitchen table until George returned.

"How's your mom?" He pulled out a chair and sat down across from me.

"Safe."

"Not in the canyon?"

I shook my head. "Zalo has a bolt-hole in the desert. We spent some time with her there."

"Have you figured out what's going on?"

"We're closer. Mom finally shared more information about Patterson."

"And I spoke with some elders in Mexico," Zalo said. "We think we know who the Magician and Patterson are. Or were."

"The problem is, we still don't know what Patterson wants. It may have something to do with the vortexes in this area."

George gave a skeptical-sounding grunt. "Mostly a bunch of tourist bunk, but there is something...something spiritual about certain places in the desert. Our tribe has known about those places for a thousand years."

"So there are some real vortexes?" I asked. My voice rose along with the speed of my heart.

He nodded. "What have you learned about Patterson?"

Zalo slurped his coffee and then huffed out a breath. "The guy's been around a long time."

"My mom has been following Patterson since he murdered my…father." I gulped down the choking feeling and pushed out the words. "I spent the night on your computer, searching through online records."

"Patterson had at least two names before he knew my parents, and who knows how many more before then? He's had at least four more in the past twelve years. I'm trying to dig further back, but it's tougher to track someone before computers." I blew out a quick breath to settle my pounding pulse. "I've checked old newspapers and census data, but he's slippery. He changes names often, and believable disguises seem to be one of his talents."

"He's very powerful. Very old," Zalo added. "I think he wants something the Magician has."

I stood and checked out the view from the small kitchen window. A thick layer of snow covered the road and clung to the trees. I gnawed on my fingernail and swallowed the sick feeling in my throat. "Or someone."

George looked slightly green around the mouth. He frowned. "When's Josh coming back?"

"He was supposed to be here by now, but with this weather, he's probably stuck in Jerome."

"He was going to get the necklace." Zalo added.

George's frown deepened, and he looked even

more worried. "In Jerome?"

I nodded, but a bone-shaking chill washed over me, and I rubbed my hands up and down my arms to get rid of the goosebumps.

George stared at the floor for a minute, decided something, and then pretended to be unconcerned. "You two look exhausted. Want some breakfast?"

"No, thanks. I'll wait until Josh gets back," I said, going for nonchalant, but my stomach did another strange flip. I smoothed my hands over the table. Why had George changed the subject? Should I read what the old man was thinking now, or wait until a more subtle moment, when he wouldn't catch me prying?

I tapped my fingers against my thigh a couple of times. Sooner rather than later struck me as a good idea, so I rubbed my hands together and waited.

George stood and peeked out the window. "The snow will melt in the valley by midmorning, although it may take longer near the top of the mountain."

Zalo gave me an eye-shift signal, and I raised my hand to catch a read, but George turned to face me too quickly. I fiddled with my hair and avoided Zalo's frustrated glance.

"More coffee?" George reached for the old percolator.

"I'm fine for now." I went back to the office. I still had documents to print. George was awake, so I set the printer to work and returned to the kitchen.

Hunched over the table, Zalo plowed through a mega-sized bowl of rainbow-colored cereal. George paced. I collated the data I'd collected and wondered which avenue I should investigate next. This process would go much faster if I had access to the face recognition software Grady used at the station, but there was no way to explain to the cops what we were up to.

With the ugly weather, it hardly seemed worth opening up the Trading Post, but George unlocked the door at nine and turned on the lights in the main store. Still frustrated with the turtle speed of my investigation, I wandered over to the display of Native artifacts locked behind glass and studied the designs on some of the beautiful pots and baskets. None of them looked anything like the cat necklace or Josh's ugly little pot.

The phone rang once in the next room, and George answered it. He spoke softly, so I couldn't hear much, but then he walked over to me and touched his hand to my shoulder. I turned. His eyes looked glassy, and his face was as gray as his braids.

My pulse shot up.

He took my hand. "There's been an accident."

My heart stopped, and my breath with it.

CHAPTER 14

Tears glittered in the old man's eyes, and then in mine. I couldn't speak, but I managed to form his name with my lips. "Josh?"

"We need to get to the hospital," George continued as he shoved arms into his coat and dug for his keys.

I don't know how I kept breathing. Fear for Josh crushed my heart and lungs. The ceiling and floor swung in dizzying directions, like I was doing loop-the-loops on the swings in the park.

George must have handed me my coat, and he and Zalo helped me into the wide front seat of the truck. I can't remember much about the ride to the hospital, except that bright yellow sunshine bouncing off the white snow blinded me at times. Or maybe those were my tears?

I breathed as deeply as I could and squeezed Zalo's hand. I had to keep calm, had to think clearly if I was going to help Josh.

I was almost sane again by the time we walked through the emergency room doors and made our way down the gleaming tile hall to the nurses' station. George knew the lady working behind the counter.

He spoke to her quietly in Yavapai. She responded and seated us in a too-bright and cheery waiting room. She spoke some words, but I don't remember what they were.

I stared out the window at the snow until Gran

160

showed up. George must have called her, because I didn't have any words yet. I guess a neighbor drove her down from Jerome.

More tears. She held onto me, but soon I was cried out. Totally numb.

The doctor walked into the waiting room in his green scrubs. The smell of anesthetic, and even the putrid green color of his clothes made my stomach lurch. I listened carefully to what he was saying, but couldn't put his words together so they made sense

Unconscious. Car accident. Head injury. Blood loss. Too many hours alone in the cold. Might be days. His expression was serious, and I clearly read the worry in his mind.

Little hope. Little hope.

I pulled myself together enough to ask, "Can we see him?"

The doctor mumbled something about later, when Josh was stabilized and out of the recovery room.

I sat on the plastic furniture and stared out the window again. George was right. The snow had already melted, and only a few mounded patches remained. I watched them disappear in the bright sunlight.

Gran wanted me to eat something. She brought me a sandwich, but when I swallowed the first bite, I ran to the bathroom and was sick.

My head cleared after I washed my face and rinsed my mouth. I came out of the bathroom and quietly sat down next to George. I leaned over to whisper in his ear. "He did this."

"Who?" he asked, but I think he already knew who I meant. His eyes narrowed to dark slits of pain and anger.

161

"Patterson," I barely mouthed the name. I glanced overhead at the security camera. A shiver of paranoia washed over me, and I cringed. Could he spy on us even in here?

Footsteps approached, and I saw Grady and Manny walking down the hall toward us. They moved in unison somehow, steps together, expressions the same. Angry determination flowed between them, and flowed into me.

When I stood, Grady folded me into her embrace. Manny put his arm around George, and we held on to each other for a while, finding reassurance and strength in being together.

I brushed away the stupid tears leaking down my face again. "Do you know anything more? The doctor didn't even know where on that stupid road the accident happened."

"What road?" Manny asked.

"The road to Jerome."

I saw their confusion, and my heart started hammering again. "Josh was headed for Jerome," I explained. "He was going to get…to pick something up…and then come back to Verde."

Manny rubbed his thumb and fingers down both sides of his mouth. "He wasn't anywhere near Jerome. He rolled the Volkswagen out on the desert road just past the old gas station. They found him down in a gully."

"He wasn't discovered until morning," Grady added. "A dump truck driver noticed him upside down in an arroyo. He tried to help Josh, but when he couldn't reach him, he drove down to the gas station and called 911."

"The gas station...but that's near..." I shut my mouth quickly and breathed through my nose until I could focus again. Manny didn't notice my mistake.

Grady did. She gently led me over to the couch and sat down next to me. "What was he doing out there, Forrest?" she asked.

I shook my head and stared at my hands, shivering with cold and fear.

"Forrest?" Grady's tone grew less friendly, more cop-like.

"I don't know. He was supposed to drive up to Jerome, supposed to...talk to my gran. Tell her where we were."

Grady shot me a slant-eyed stare.

Face it, I'm a terrible liar. I fiddled with the edge of my jacket, because I couldn't look her in the eye, but even I knew the move was a totally obvious tell.

"Why didn't you just call your gran?" she drilled down for the truth. "Why did Josh go out on a dangerous night when you could have just..."

"You two are in trouble again, aren't you?" Manny interrupted.

I swallowed hard and tucked my chin.

Manny knelt down and, with one finger, gently tipped my face up until I had no choice but to look at him. He didn't seem angry, just totally worried. "Does this have to do with your mother?"

Gran must have heard his question, because she sucked in a quick breath. "Your mother? Forrest, what does he mean?"

I shot Manny a disgusted look. "Big mouth."

"Is Angela here? Where is she? Is she safe?" Gran's voice grew more and more shrill with every question.

I took her hands and pulled her down on the opposite side of the couch. "Gran, I'll explain in a minute."

George sat down next to her. "Let me. Then you can answer the other questions." George took Gran by the arm and gently led her off to another corner of the waiting room. He spoke to her in hushed tones.

I was so, so tired. My whole body ached like I'd run for hundreds of miles, and all I wanted to do was sleep, but I had two angry cops waiting for answers. I wasn't going to tell them where Mom was hiding, but I could explain the rest of the story. Hopefully, Manny would understand.

I gave them the cliff notes version:

My mother, the condemned murder, was trying to prove her innocence. An ancient and powerful spirit-slash-human threatened her and us, and had been spying on us. The creep was wealthy, connected, powerful, and downright evil. Zalo had figured out he was an ancient enemy of the....

Manny gave me the fisheye when I almost mentioned the stupid ghost.

I pulled back. "I mean the enemy of Josh. He wants something, and we think it might be the necklace."

Grady's eyes got round with disbelief, but when Manny didn't react to the crazy, mixed-up story with anything but a few brief questions, I think she began to believe me.

"The necklace Josh found? The one in the museum?" Grady stared at her boots for a moment, and I could see she was sorting all these new facts in her mind. It wouldn't take long before she'd piece the whole story together.

"Is the necklace powerful?" she asked quietly.

Manny and I must have both gasped at the same time.

"Humm. Thought so." Grady rose and paced the linoleum in front of us, rubbing her finger across her brow.

"How'd you know?" I asked her.

"I've read a few legends myself." She glanced over at Manny. "And I've suspected a few people weren't telling me the whole truth."

Manny gave a sheepish shrug.

Grady crossed her arms. "Spill it, Gutierrez."

Manny stood and held up his hands in surrender. "I will, I promise. You deserve to know, but now isn't the time." He glanced around the waiting room filled with several families. "Or the place."

Grady's pinched her lips into a tight grimace, but then she nodded.

Manny sat down next to me on the chair. "How's Josh doing?"

I glanced over at the ominous closed doors of the ICU. "Not good."

****

Living in a hospital waiting room is hell. Gran tried to get me to go home for a few hours to sleep, but she finally gave up when George took my side. They brought me food, and water, and a change of clothes. I slept on the sofa the first night.

In the morning, I washed in the ladies' bathroom and choked down a stale bagel from the hospital cafeteria. We were allowed into the ICU for five minutes every two hours, so we took turns. Sometimes

George went, sometimes I did.

Zalo took off early that morning, but returned after evening rounds. He must have been watching, because when Grady left about nine the second night, he slipped in like a...ghost. I almost smiled at the thought.

"Did you talk to my mom?" I asked after he gave me a hug. "She must be frantic. We were supposed to be back at the cabin yesterday."

He nodded. "I saw her."

"You can't let Mom come here. It won't do any good."

"Wasn't easy to leave alone. I promised to report back."

I glanced up at the clock. Two minutes to the hour, and my turn to see Josh. "I need to go in."

"I'll check back later," Zalo said.

I grabbed his hand. "Maybe they'll let you come in, too. The night nurse is a little more understanding than the dragon lady who guards the ward during the day."

We peeked into the ICU, and I pulled Zalo through the door after me. I quickly moved to Josh's alcove. I'd almost gotten used to the beep-beeping of the machines, and the flashing lights monitoring Josh's blood pressure and heart rate.

His nurse smiled at me. "He's doing fine. No change, but no worse."

"This is his friend. Is it okay?"

The nurse patted my arm. "It won't do Josh any harm, but just for a minute, dear. Talk to him. Let him know you're here."

The bandages still covered the bruised part of Josh's forehead, but the doctor had removed the breathing tube this morning.

I took his limp hand and squeezed it tightly. Zalo stood on the other side of the bed. He shuffled, and he looked everywhere but at Josh. He looked miserable.

"Do you want to leave?" I asked him.

Zalo shook his head.

I took a second to see Zalo's thoughts.

A vision of an old woman lying in a hospital bed. The monitor nearby traced a straight line across the screen. Zalo stood nearby, alone.

I swallowed quickly and lowered my hand. Poor kid.

I sat down in the chair so I could be right next to Josh's ear. Even if he could really hear me, I needed to speak quietly. "Josh," I whispered. "The nurse says I'm supposed to talk to you, so here goes. If you can hear me, maybe you can let me know."

Josh remained motionless, and my throat tightened up. The words got tough to say. I blinked a couple of times before I could speak again. "I don't know what to do, Colonel Mustard. You said you were going to Jerome, but you didn't. How can I help you? Do you need the necklace?"

A cold swoosh of frigid air blew across my face, and I shivered. I glanced across at Zalo. His dark eyes were big and round. His mouth hung open.

"What?" I whispered, and he pointed to the corner of the room behind me. I turned, but there was nothing there.

Zalo's face was ashen. "The Magician. He was just…"

I kept hold of Josh's hand and said again, "How can I help you, Josh?"

I watched. There. My heart started pounding. I

could see the ghost, too. A vision hovered in the corner.

I'd seen the Magician before, on the cliff edge when we trapped Sheriff Robb. The bitter cold reached out to me, surrounded me. I shivered, but opened my thoughts. The Magician could help Josh, if only I could understand him.

I closed my eyes and saw the necklace and the ugly pot Josh had brought to Zalo. A lilting bar of music played, and I remembered the courting flute. When opened my eyes, the Magician was gone.

"Okay, he told me," I whispered to Zalo. "I know what to do."

Zalo shivered once more and bolted for the door. "Tell me outside."

****

George called Grady and asked her to bring coffee. It only took ten minutes for her to show up at the hospital. Manny followed her through the door.

"Lights and sirens," Manny said before I asked. "Coffee was the signal, right?"

"Forrest knows how to help Josh," Zalo blurted before I could get the words out.

"How?"

I turned my back on the security camera. "The Magician told me." I waved everyone to the back corner of the waiting room where we could speak freely, away from the prying eyes of the security cam.

Since it was Friday, there were few surgeries, so the place was empty. I faced away from the security camera again and lowered my voice to a whisper. Paranoia is brutal, but I wasn't going to take any more chances with Josh's life.

"We need to get the Magician's tools together. He

can help Josh."

"What do we need?" Manny dug out his uber-phone to take notes, but I hesitated before listing the items.

"Paper only." I pointed to the phone. Manny nodded, stashed it, and found a beat up notepad from his coat pocket.

"We need the pot Josh found during the flood." I continued. "Grady, could you get that? I hope it's still in his pack. He had it with him when he crashed the V-dub."

Grady nodded "I'll ask the nurse to see his possessions."

"We need the flute, too." I continued. "It's at Gina' and Rocky's place."

"I could call Rocky." Manny offered.

"No," we all shouted at once. "No more phone calls."

Grady and Manny exchanged suspicious glances.

"It was dangerous enough to get you here to the hospital," I continued. "Please. We have to go get it, but, if possible, Rocky and Gina can't know."

Manny rubbed his chin and nodded.

"What about the necklace?" Zalo asked under his breath.

"Yes. We can get that, too. Manny, can you take me to the museum after we stop at Rocky's?"

"I want to help," said Zalo.

"Can you go get my mother?"

Looking confused, then scared, Zalo glanced at the cops.

"She needs to be here. We all do."

"Done," Zalo said.

George and my gran walked into the waiting room, looking curious about our convention in the back of the room.

"Come on," Zalo ordered the old man. "I need a ride." Zalo practically shoved George out the door.

Suddenly I felt lighter than I had in days. The pressure in my chest eased, and I could pull a deep breath. There was hope. We could save Josh. The Magician would help us, and then we would help him.

"Thank you," I whispered.

Grady studied my face, and then moved on to study each of the others in the group. "I'll stay here. Josh will be under official police protection until you return. You can help, Angel Wings."

I hugged Grady. "Thanks. I promise we'll explain everything when we can. Just don't haul my mom off to jail if she arrives before Manny and I return."

Next I gave Gran a quick hug, grabbed my coat, and turned just in time to see Manny give Grady a quick kiss. Hah! I knew it.

Manny drove like a grandma. No, I take that back. He drove like a great grandma. It was all I could do not to jump out of the car and run to the museum. It would have been faster.

Finally, we rounded the last curve into Jerome, and I let out a relieved sigh. We parked down the street from Rocky's Roost.

"Do you know where the flute is?" Manny asked.

"Used to." I told him about the bookcase in Rocky's living room.

"I'll keep Rocky and Gina busy in the bar. You go around the back way. They never lock their place."

Icy patches still covered the ground at this

elevation. I slipped once and landed on my butt, but hurried down the steep alley as fast as I could. Manny was right. The side door was open, and I slipped inside. I found the flute behind the dusty copy of Moby Dick and stuck it inside my coat.

I was back in the car before Manny came through the front door of the bar. I ducked down to hide. Simpler that way. If Rocky or Gina saw me from the window, we'd have to deal with more questions.

Manny jumped back in the driver's seat and reported, "Rocky and Gina plan to visit Josh again tomorrow."

"Good. He'll be awake by then."

We drove over to the History Museum. I waved to the priest sitting on the front steps of the old Catholic church, and he waved back. Pretty cold to be sitting outside, but he looked comfortable in the sunshine.

Manny led the way up the wooden steps and into the warm entrance of the museum. I glanced around. In the next room, the necklace gleamed in its locked and lighted case. I rubbed my cold hands together. If only I had a baseball bat, we'd be out of here in no time.

Manny flashed his badge and explained we needed to secure the necklace. The ticket-taker called the manager, and the manager called the director. Every call made me more nervous. Would Patterson find out we were after the necklace? I chewed on my nonexistent fingernails and looked around for that baseball bat.

The thin-lipped director entered the room. She recognized me and almost smiled. Manny took her aside and spoke to her quietly. Eventually she dug out her keys and handed over the necklace.

171

"You understand," she said through her nose, "you take full responsibility."

We were out the door before she could finish her warning. I ran to the car and jumped in the passenger side. "How...."

"Charm." he grinned at me. "And the threat of a court order."

I buckled in. "Whatever it takes."

****

Mom finally arrived at the hospital. George's four-wheel drive truck pulled up to the front entrance, and George, Zalo, and my mother climbed out.

She hurried inside and gathered me up in her arms. "I've been so worried."

"Thanks for coming, Mom. I know this is a huge risk."

She brushed my hair back from my face and tipped up my chin. "We can't keep hiding. And we have to help Josh."

Grady gave my mom the once-over, but then relaxed.

Mom went over and took Grady's hand. "Thank you so much for helping my daughter. You can't know how much I appreciate what you've done for her."

Grady blushed and dropped her eyes. "We can deal with the details later."

Manny pushed through the heavy ICU doors and waved us all forward. Fortunately, the dragon lady was off duty today.

We tiptoed in. Only one other bed on the opposite side of the ICU was occupied, and that patient was alone and asleep.

We each found a place near Josh, and the nurse

closed the flimsy blue curtains to give us some privacy. I don't know what I expected, but my hands shook as I reached inside my coat and pulled out the flute. I closed Josh's fingers around the small instrument.

Grady placed the water pot near Josh's other hand.

Manny held out the necklace. "What should I do?"

"Place it on his chest."

I glanced around the room, waiting for Magician to appear. I counted the seconds with my pounding heartbeats and check again. Nothing. My vision blurred.

"Forrest?" whispered my mother.

"Something's not right," I said. "The Magician didn't come. He should…"

Manny cursed under his breath. "He should have shown by now." Manny took the necklace and carefully examined it under the bright light near Josh's bed. The monitors beeped while we all held our breath.

"It's a fake," he announced.

My knees gave out. I don't remember walking back to the waiting room. Next thing I knew, my mother was patting my hand while Grady pressed a cold towel against my forehead.

"I was so sure," I moaned. "I was so sure my plan would work."

Manny paced the long hallway and then stopped in front of me. He held the necklace in his hands. "Do you know who could have replaced the real one with this fake?"

I shook my head.

"Could it be Patterson?" my mother asked.

George turned from his place near the window. "Josh and I did it," he confessed. His face caved in.

I jumped up. "Why didn't you tell us?"

173

Grady grabbed hold of me, and it was all I could do to keep from pummeling him with my fists.

George held up his hands, palms out. "I'm sorry. Zalo pushed me out the door. I didn't know what you were planning until we all stood around his bed."

"Where is it?" I demanded.

"I don't know." He looked even more miserable. "Josh was the only one who knew. It was safer that way."

Manny took me by the shoulders and turned me around to face him. "Is there any place Josh has taken you, a secret place, where he might have hidden the real necklace?"

My eyes must have opened wider. I know my face went pale, because I could feel the blood drop from my head to my stomach, and I sat down hard on the chair.

"You know, don't you?" Grady knelt in front of me. "I can go get it. Or Manny can."

"No," Manny chimed in. "This is something Forrest has to do."

I felt cold, then hot, then cold again. I couldn't stop shaking. I couldn't go into the salt mine again, but I had no choice. "You'd never find it. I'm not sure I can."

I glanced at the half circle of worried adults. "Mom?" I choked out the words. "Can you take me?"

George handed her the keys to his truck without being asked.

Grady frowned, but Manny put a hand out. "Cool it, Grady. You know they're coming back."

With her arm around my shoulder, Mom and I hurried through the hospital doors and into the late afternoon light. We would have to hurry if we were going to find the salt mines before dark.

174

CHAPTER 15

Mom drove. I held on. My knuckles ached.

We passed the gas station and raced down the long, empty road. I watched the desert landscape fly by and chewed on my lip. My stomach knotted. How would I find the mines again? Josh and I had cut across the desert the one time he brought me there. Could I even find the place, much less face going back inside that horrible cave?

Sunset threw ominous shadows across the desert.

"Hurry," I whispered, bracing myself.

Mom drove faster, screeching around the corners on the narrow, bumpy road.

"Wait," I shouted, my heart thumping more quickly in my chest.

She slowed the truck.

"There. See the old No Trespassing sign?' There were signs just like that at the mine."

She stopped the truck on the gravel shoulder of the road near a gang of many-armed Saguaros.

I jumped out and zipped up my jacket. The wind felt icy, and the clouds rushed over us, gray and ominous, allowing only hints of cold sunlight.

"We'll have to hike the rest of the way." I shoved on the mittens that lived in my pockets.

Mom shrugged into her coat and grabbed a flashlight. I found one in George's glove compartment.

We helped each other through the barbed wire

175

fence. I was practically running, but slowed as the hill got steeper. Mom followed, doing her best to keep up. At the top I searched the open desert around me, searching for a landmark I could recognize.

The spiny points of the ocotillos cast long, black shadows across the rocky hillside. Down below, I saw the dry arroyo Josh and I had crossed. Another hundred yards farther on were the mines' boarded-over openings.

"There," I shouted, suddenly filled with hope.

We skidded down the hill. Late evening light glowed against the crystals of salt. I knelt to pull at the old boards covering the shaft. One by one, I ripped them loose, and Mom tossed them aside.

I licked my lips and turned on the flashlight. "I think I can find it. Josh only took me into the first open room. He had the necklace hidden down one of the tunnels."

"I'll come, too."

"Maybe you should stay out here. If one of the tunnels collapsed, you'll need to go for help."

Mom got a stubborn look on her face, just like the one Gran gets when I've blown it somehow. "I'll come too," she repeated.

I didn't argue. Truth? I was scared shitless. A little company in the spooky old place wasn't such a terrible idea. Even though my heart raced in my throat, I sucked up my courage and crawled into the narrow tunnel.

"Stay right by my feet. It's about fifty feet to the open space," I called back to Mom.

She grunted her way down the tunnel behind me, and soon we entered the crystal room. I rose to my hands and knees, crawled over to dig in Josh's supplies, and found each of us a bottle of water. Josh had extra flashlights, and I handed another one to Mom.

"Which way now?" she asked, after downing half a bottle of water.

"There. Josh went down that tunnel." I shoved aside a few of the rocks blocking the way. "See the little plastic tag? That's got to be his marker."

I poked my head into the even narrower tunnel, shining the light as far back as it would go.

"Josh said there were a couple of turns." I closed my eyes, trying to remember, but I still wasn't sure I recalled his words correctly.

"Should I follow you?"

"No, I think it's better if you stay here. Call to me every few minutes, and I'll answer back. That way I can keep my directions straight. If I can't find the treasure, I'll come back out and try again."

I took a last gulp of water, tied my hair back in a scrunchie and lay down flat on my stomach. There was barely room to maneuver through the first part of the tunnel. I had to turn and twist to make it through.

Water dripped somewhere, and my hands felt wet as I pushed along the walls, but soon my mouth and eyes and nose were gritty with the salty dust. Rotted beams covered the floor in places. The beam of the flashlight shot spooky shadows over the fallen rocks blocking the way down the path to the right.

"Not that way." I said to myself. Even my whisper sounded deafening in the small space.

I turned left, but the tunnel narrowed, and I froze, unable to move forward. My heart pounded, and I tried to scoot back, but couldn't. An icy feeling of panic rushed over me, and I cried out. My quick breaths fogged the small space.

The darkness smothered me.

No.

I closed my eyes and sucked in stale air through my nose. I had to do this. No choice. I had to. For Josh. I gritted my teeth and pushed my toes against the wall, finally inching forward again.

"Forrest?" Mom called behind me.

"Doing fine," I lied cheerfully.

My flashlight shook in my hand, but I examined each of the tunnels that flowed from the main path. One seemed much less cluttered with debris, like someone had crawled through here many times. I almost smiled. Even if he didn't realize it, Josh had left me a clue. I scooted down the cleared path and squeezed through another tight spot.

Mom voice seemed much farther away when she called my name this time, but I returned her signal.

Which way now? I reached up to feel for the rock overhead. The ceiling was higher than it had been in quite a while, and I could sit up. I crossed my legs and glanced around, carefully examining the crystalized space with my light. I clamped my jaw shut to stop my teeth from chattering, then closed my eyes and thought about Josh sitting next to me, and my heart and breath slowed.

Right now I wished I had Josh's talent for touching things. I bet he could touch a rock and follow a trail. He'd know which way to go, just like a bloodhound.

I set my teeth and studied each corner of the tiny space. There. To my left, the shadow of a rock cairn danced against the wall. I crawled toward it.

I pushed aside the rocks and dug in the soft sand

under them. My fingers touched a cold hard surface, and my heart started to race even faster.

Mom called again, her voice more faint and echo-like. I yelled as loudly as I could to make sure she heard.

I pulled the box out of the hole, and my joyful shout echoed in the space. I peeked inside and saw the gleaming eyes of the cat.

Sneaky guy. When had Josh replaced the necklace? Had he ever taken the real one out of the mine?

It only took a few moments for me to make the return trip. "Marco," I shouted to the dim light ahead of me.

"Polo." My mom's laughter filled the tunnel. I hadn't heard that sound since I was four, and I suddenly remembered her holding me and laughing. I choked back the tears, emerged from the tunnel, and fell into her arms.

"I have it."

"I'm so proud of you, Forrest. You used to be afraid of the dark."

I glanced over my shoulder and shivered. "Still am."

I bent to brush the salt dust off my clothes and almost fell into the ghost. I gave a sharp scream, but more from surprise than fear.

Mom clutched my shoulder. "Forrest, what is it?"

The spook stood before me, dressed in his red cloak. I looked into his steady, life-like gaze and recognized the boy I loved. They had the same amber-colored eyes.

"Can't you see him?" I whispered.

"Who?"

"Guess not." I cleared my throat. "Josh's ghost is right here in front of us.

Mom took a step back.

"He won't hurt us."

I held up the box and showed the Magician his necklace. "I need to help Josh. Please. Come with me."

He nodded, turned into the dark, and was gone.

"Is he still here?" My mom hissed.

I shook my head. "Let's go. He'll meet us there."

"Are you sure?" she asked as we crawled into the fresh evening air.

"Yes, but there isn't much time."

"How do you know?"

"The ghost just told me."

****

Walking across the desert in the dark is tough. On a moonless night, it's almost impossible. Even with our flashlights, we got lost and had to hunt for the truck. I had to pull Mom away from the cholla cactus twice, but we finally found the many-armed saguaros near where we'd parked.

Finally, finally we were back on the road. I was shaking too hard, so Mom had to drive the truck.

Funny thing. She drove so fast I had to close my eyes and hold on. Must run in the family. I almost laughed as she pulled up in front of the hospital with a screech of tires.

I turned to jump out of the truck, but Mom grabbed my hand. "Forrest. I know you're full of hope right now."

"Don't say it, Mom."

"I just…I just want you to know I love you."

I smiled and then grinned at her. "Love you too,

Mom. Come on. We have a ghost waiting for us."

****

I could feel the Magician's presence the moment we walked into the room. I couldn't see him, but I knew he was close by. Even though the room felt like a walk-in-freezer, nobody seemed to notice but me.

We gathered around the bed and replaced the objects the Magician would use to save Josh. I placed the real cat necklace on Josh's chest, and I could see him softly breathing beneath it. My heart raced like Tilley on an uphill climb. "Please, oh please," I said under my breath.

We waited. I glanced around, but no ghost appeared. I gulped back the sick feeling that pushed up from my stomach. "You can't let Josh down now, you old spook," I shouted at the blue curtains.

"Forrest, honey. Do you want us to wait outside?"

I brushed my cheek with the back of my hand and realized my face was wet. I turned to my mother. "I was so sure…I mean, it was supposed to work. How…?"

"We'll leave you alone with Josh for a minute." She kissed me on the cheek and led the others out the door.

I rubbed my face with my hands and sucked in a deep breath to calm myself. Why? Why hadn't my plan worked? I'd been so sure the Magician would help Josh. "Stupid ghost. If Josh doesn't wake up soon, the doctors say he might never wake up. Then what will you do?"

A cold draft brushed across my face and surrounded me. I froze, not from the cold, but from excitement. "Show yourself, you damned old spook."

One moment the curtains across from me were just

curtains, the next, an ancient shaman stood in front of them. I caught my breath. "What took you so long?"

He almost smiled.

No, I swear. He did.

A strange purple-white light filled the room, and drums echoed from somewhere, everywhere. The ghost stepped forward and held out a tiny woven basket.

I took it in my hands. It weighed nothing, but was beautifully made, exquisite. I placed it on Josh's stomach, just below the necklace. The light dimmed, the drums faded, and when I looked up again, the ghost was gone. "Thank you." I whispered.

I sat down next to Josh and waited. Was it a minute, or an hour? I couldn't say, but then his eyes flickered, and he drew a deeper breath. Josh stirred, stretched, and opened his eyes, like he'd just taken an afternoon nap.

"Hey," he whispered. He glanced around the room and frowned, his brows drawing closer to his beautiful eyes.

"You're in the hospital." I said.

"Accident."

I nodded.

"Patterson."

"Tell me."

CHAPTER 16

Manny marched into my hospital room and folded his arms in disgust. "Patterson's still missing."

Grady followed the sergeant into the room and shushed him before closing the door. "We don't want the world to know about this yet. Not until we track the guy down and get him in custody."

"Never will. Not now." The cop grumbled and stared out the window.

"Why not?" I asked. "I can testify against him anytime. He ran me off the road."

"He knows we're on to him. He's gone into hiding," Grady explained.

Forrest walked into the room, a bunch of autumn flowers in her arms. They lit up her face with color, and she smiled to see me sitting in the chair instead of laid out in bed. She glanced over at Manny's dejected expression. "What's up?" she asked.

"Patterson. He booked it," I said.

"Nobody's seen him since about the time Josh woke up," Grady explained.

"It'll be a big stink." Manny spread his arms like he was reading the headlines. "State Representative Missing for Six Days."

"Better for us," I pointed out. "He'll be easier to track."

Forrest set the flowers on the bedside table. "I never could figure out why he took such a high-profile position this time."

Grady dragged a chair over and sat down in front of me. "Josh. Are you ready to make your statement?"

"Yeah, I haven't had a headache most of the day. No meds, so I can mostly remember what happened."

Forrest hovered next to me, and I reached up to take her hand. "Let's get this over with."

Grady swiped a button on her digital recorder and did the legal thing.

I took a sip of water and began the story. "I went to get the necklace, the real one, the night it snowed. George had a craftsman up on the Hopi rez make a duplicate several years ago. We knew there would come a time when we'd have to bring the cat out into the modern world, but we didn't want to take a risk of someone stealing it. It's too powerful. The real one was never in the museum."

"Wasn't it authenticated by that expert?" Forrest asked. "Remember when you gave it to the museum, before we caught Robb?"

I gave her a quick shrug. "That expert? Same guy who made the fake."

"So the real necklace stayed in the salt mine all this time?" Forrest concluded.

"Yeah." I cleared my throat and noticed the hurt on Forrest's face. "Sorry."

"S'okay," she replied.

"Anyway, that night, I set off for Jerome, just in case anyone was watching the Trading Post, but I used the back way through Cottonwood to head down to the mines. I didn't think I'd been followed. By then Patterson must have figured out the necklace wasn't in the museum."

"Wouldn't he have stolen it long ago if it was real?"

"Probably," I agreed. "Anyway, I was on the mine road. The storm was at whiteout, so I stopped at the gas station." I glanced at Forrest, and she nodded.

"Patterson must have been waiting for me, or followed me there. I didn't notice him until he was right behind me."

I swallowed hard, and Forrest squeezed my hand for reassurance.

"With that big car, all he had to do was shove me off the road and down a gully." I closed my eyes and remembered the horrible feeling of losing control and flipping over and over.

"Sorry about your gran's car," I said to Forrest.

She slowly raised and lowered one shoulder. "No big deal."

Grady leaned in closer to me. "Did you see him? See Patterson's face?"

"He walked over to check out the wreck. I never saw his face, but I recognized his boots. I got the feeling, in that split second, he wanted me to know he was going to kill me, and there was nothing I could do about it. He had a gun."

I wanted Forrest to see the whole truth, so I lowered my barriers. She shivered next to me, but she saw the truth and understood the Magician had saved me more than once.

There was room in the chair for both of us, so I pulled her down, and she cuddled in under my arm. She felt so good next to me. "How did you figure out about the necklace?" I asked her.

"The museum fake didn't work. We tried it. Your

ghost wouldn't come." She cuddled closer, and I kissed her on the temple. "George admitted the necklace was a repro."

"And then you went to the mine to find the real one? You hate that place."

"Yes. I. Do," Forrest answered emphatically.

I chuckled. "But you went anyway. Down that rabbit hole?"

She turned and kissed me on the lips, in front of the cops. Don't get me wrong...I didn't mind. I touched her face and smoothed my hand down her beautiful hair.

"But Josh." She pulled back a fraction.

I opened my eyes from the kiss. "Yeah?"

"Don't ask me to do it again."

Grady had a few more questions, and then the cops took off. Forrest was still cuddled under my arm, and we relaxed into each other.

I felt warm, safe. "Doc says I can go home tomorrow."

"That's great. You'll be back on the cross-county team in no time."

"What about your mom?"

"When Patterson disappeared, the cops got a warrant to go through his stuff. He'd destroyed most of it, but one or two documents were still in his safe."

"He was in a pretty big hurry."

"The FBI's all over it now. He had a very sophisticated listening setup. Guess he was spying on all sorts of people. Even had a listening device in the governor's office. That's probably how he knew you were out on that road. He'd tapped into all the highway cameras."

I let out a long whistle.

"Soooo, Grady sat on the DA until he went through every detail, even the information on Patterson that my mom and I hacked. They found enough evidenced to free my mom. She's out on bail right now, but Manny is sure the case against her will be dropped."

"That's great."

She nodded into my shoulder. "My gran is so happy. She goes around the apartment humming and smiling. Mom's staying with us for now."

"Forrest?" I whispered in her ear.

"Hummm?"

"Remember what I told you before I left?"

Her body tensed. She sat up and stared at me, her face guarded.

"I wanted..." I stumbled over my words and drew in another breath to start again.

She drew her hands back with a hesitant frown. "You want to take it back? I get it. Call it the heat of the moment? Whatever...."

"No. No. Wait. Of course I love you. I fell for you that first day, when we met by the river."

She smiled, and I felt that wonderful, dazzled feeling of being lost in her blue-green eyes.

"I love you too."

I skimmed my hand down her soft cheek. "Some events are still a little fuzzy. I can't tell what was really happening and what I was dreaming. I have these weird images of the Magician standing over me. He brought me a basket." I searched her face for the truth. "You were crying."

A new tear trickled down her face, and I leaned over to kiss it away.

"Here." She pulled something from her pocket. "I

kept it safe until you were well." She placed a tiny basket in my hands. "The Magician brought it the night you woke up."

"It's the seed basket—another one of his tools."

"Figured that. What's it for?

"I don't know yet, but the Magician will teach me."

A word about the author...

Along with teaching, Joy began her writing career by publishing children's historical fiction. She later found writing romantic suspense fulfilled her need for travel and romance. Joy grew up in Arizona and always felt a special affinity for the haunts of the central part of the state. She lives with her husband and two dogs near Silicon Valley and the mythical town of Sereno.
http://www.ejbrighton.com

Thank you for purchasing
this publication of The Wild Rose Press, Inc.

For questions or more information
contact us at
info@thewildrosepress.com.

The Wild Rose Press, Inc.
www.thewildrosepress.com